SPECIAL MESSAGE TO READERS

This book is published under the auspices of

THE ULVERSCROFT FOUNDATION

(registered charity No. 264873 UK)

Established in 1972 to provide funds for research, diagnosis and treatment of eye diseases. Examples of contributions made are: —

A Children's Assessment Unit at Moorfield's Hospital, London.

•

Twin operating theatres at the Western Ophthalmic Hospital, London.

•

A Chair of Ophthalmology at the Royal Australian College of Ophthalmologists.

•

The Ulverscroft Children's Eye Unit at the Great Ormond Street Hospital For Sick Children, London.

You can help further the work of the Foundation by making a donation or leaving a legacy. Every contribution, no matter how small, is received with gratitude. Please write for details to:

THE ULVERSCROFT FOUNDATION,
The Green, Bradgate Road, Anstey,
Leicester LE7 7FU, England.
Telephone: (0116) 236 4325

In Australia write to:

THE ULVERSCROFT FOUNDATION,
c/o The Royal Australian and New Zealand
College of Ophthalmologists,
94-98 Chalmers Street, Surry Hills,
N.S.W. 2010, Australia

GUN LAW

Aged fourteen, Jake Chalmers witnessed his parents' murder by drunken cowboys. Now he's a young man — with a gun for protection . . . On the run after killing, in self-defence, Jake arrives in Sweetwater. But he's unable to maintain a low profile when he becomes embroiled in a feud between the businessman Jordan Carter, and sheriff Luke Gardner. Then one of Carter's men murders Luke, and Jake must choose between the law of the land and the law of the gun . . .

LEE WALKER

GUN LAW

Complete and Unabridged

LINFORD
Leicester

First published in Great Britain in 2009 by
Robert Hale Limited
London

First Linford Edition
published 2010
by arrangement with
Robert Hale Limited
London

British Library CIP Data

Walker, Lee, *1963* –
Gun law.- -(Linford western stories)
1. Western stories.
2. Large type books.
I. Title II. Series
823.9′2–dc22

ISBN 978–1–44480–401–0

Published by
F. A. Thorpe (Publishing)
Anstey, Leicestershire

Set by Words & Graphics Ltd.
Anstey, Leicestershire
Printed and bound in Great Britain by
T. J. International Ltd., Padstow, Cornwall

This book is printed on acid-free paper

For Rosie

1

At his corner table in the Broken Arrow saloon, Jake Chalmers had been hoping his one night's stay in Winters Creek would be no more exciting than a couple of cool beers and a quiet game of poker. Now it looked as though it might not turn out that way.

Although it was early evening, the saloon was already busy. It was noisy, smoky and filled with teams of cowhands just arrived from the end of their punishing trail drive. With serious drinking time to catch up on, they were wasting no time in getting down to it. Most of the hard-earned greenbacks, which were burning holes in their canvas pants, would soon be spent on hard liquor and poker or blackjack. What was left would be parted from them by the saloon girls, hovering around the room like pretty moths in the dim kerosene lamps that did their best to pierce the heavy clouds of tobacco smoke.

Standing two deep at the bar, the men shared tall tales and low jokes and enjoyed the relief from the dust, constant danger and just plain hard grind that had been their lives for most of the last three months. For now it was all just high-spirited, harmless fun, but Jake knew from bitter experience that it didn't take long for things to turn nasty in places like this.

That was why Jake had been keeping one eye on the young cowboy and the blonde soiled dove at the end of the busy bar. The boy had been declaring his undying love for the last half-hour, but for her this was purely business. She had quickly lost interest in the young wrangler, who'd been too long on the trail with only longhorns for company. There were too many other easy pickings to be had tonight and, if he wasn't spending, he was just wasting her time. Too bad the young cowboy just didn't know how to take 'no' for an answer and that spurred on by cheap bourbon and the jeers of his trail partners, the more she protested the more he persisted.

Jake watched closely as she suddenly turned her back and walked away. The young cowboy's face clouded in anger and he grabbed her by the wrist. Determined to get her attention, he roughly pushed her up against the bar and trapped her there by pressing his dusty chaps between the folds of her red dress. Angrily, she started to punch his chest with clenched fists but the boy didn't flinch. He pressed his body closer to hers until she had to swing her face away from his unshaven chin as it came ever closer, his hungry mouth seeking hers.

Suddenly, in a desperate attempt to escape, the prairie nymph lashed out with her open hand. The boy saw it coming but didn't pull away quickly enough and her painted nails gouged into his face, leaving three bloody streaks down his left check. He yelped in surprise as the pain stung him like a branding-iron. He put his fingertips to his face and gingerly felt the wounds. While he stared in disbelief at the blood on his hands, a crowd of onlookers bayed and jeered. He looked around him as though seeing the other cowboys for the first time. His heart sank as he realized he would probably never live this down. He could imagine mile after mile of dusty trail as they returned to the ranch. The story would be told and retold around the chuck wagon every night: how he had arrived in town boasting of seducing his first woman and then been bettered in a straight fight by this slip of a girl.

As he swung back to look at her, his eyes misted with anger.

'Why you dirty little whore . . . '

He lunged at her, his hand grabbing her around her throat. The girl let out a scream and fell against the bar. Reaching behind him, he pulled a long-bladed Bowie knife from the back of his gunbelt and before the girl knew what was happening, he had forced it up against her rouged cheek. Snarling like a dog, he yanked her head back with a handful of curled blonde hair.

'Ain't so sassy now, are you, Missy?' growled the boy, his face so close that white spittle flecked her face. 'Ain't good enough for you, am I? Well, if I can't have you, nobody can.'

He caressed the side of her jaw with the silver hunting blade.

'By the time I'm through with you, your mama won't even want to kiss you . . . '

His *compadres* suddenly went quiet, realizing that things had taken a nasty turn. They didn't want any trouble, at least not on their first night in town. One of the older hands stepped towards him.

'I think that's enough, Ike,' he said calmly.

'No, it ain't enough!' the boy screamed. 'Nobody's gonna make a fool of me — especially a little slut like this!'

He turned back to the whimpering girl and pressed the knife harder against her face.

'It's done when I say it's done,' he whispered.

That was when Jake rose slowly to his feet. He murmured to the dealer that he was 'out' and tossed his hand of cards into the centre of the round table. The other players gaped at the kings and nines lying on the pile of silver dollars and watched the tall, lean stranger make his way across the sawdust-covered bar room floor.

Jake pushed his way through the noisy crowd of liquored-up cowboys, ignoring the shouting, cursing and raucous singing accompanying the beat-up honky-tonk piano being banged in the corner. When he reached the bar, he tapped the young boy on the shoulder. Ike spun round, his eyes wide and wild.

'I don't think she wants your custom, son,' said Jake quietly.

Ike tightened his grip on the knife

and swallowed hard. He looked the tall stranger up and down. At first glance he looked just like most of the cowboys and drifters in the room. Even though he had called him 'son', he was not much older than Ike — he couldn't have been more than twenty-three — but his bearing and the set of his strong, determined jaw spoke of an age much older than his years. And his eyes . . . Even though they were narrowed and shaded by his black Stetson, his eyes were deep pools of black liquid. If they were the windows to his soul that was a deep and dangerous place to go.

Ike tried to draw himself up to his full height and steady his voice.

'Ain't nothin' to do with you, mister. This ain't none of your business.'

Jake looked at the boy with something akin to pity. He could see he was scared, no more than nineteen and probably just finishing his first trail drive. A boy doing a man's job, too eager to grow up and, like so many others before him, prove himself to be the toughest guy in town.

'I'm making it my business,' said Jake patiently, 'so let her go.'

Ike shook his head.

'I don't take orders from you or no one. You'd best disappear or you'll get what she's gonna get if she don't start being a whole lot nicer to me!'

He tugged again on the fistful of hair and the girl let out a yelp of fear. The sharp blade was now making a deep red line on her soft cheek though it had yet to make blood flow. Jake knew that the only way to get the girl out of this in one piece was to get the boy to hate him more than he hated her.

'Let her go,' he said again, his voice low and level.

The piano music faltered then stuttered to a halt. The deafening noise in the saloon faded to a murmur as the customers realized that the evening's entertainment was just about to liven up.

Jake sensed the change in the saloon and almost wished he'd not got involved. Now there was no easy way out for either of them. He had confronted this boy in front of his cronies in a packed bar room and he knew that only one of them would walk away. As Ike's eyes blinked nervously, he knew the boy realized it too.

Suddenly, Ike pushed the girl away. She fell against the bar heavily and slid to the floor, gasping for breath but otherwise unharmed. Ike slowly returned the Bowie into the sheaf in the back of his belt, then turned to face Jake square on. He brought his hand round to his side, fingers hovering over his holster.

'Don't do it, son,' said Jake quietly, knowing that he was trying to talk sense to someone beyond reasoning.

'Scared?' sneered the boy with a nervous smile.

Jake shook his head slowly.

'No, I'm not scared. I just don't want to kill you if I don't have to. That's all. You can still walk away. You don't need to do this. You got nothing to prove.'

The boy grinned wildly as he looked around the room. For the first time in his life he was the centre of attraction. A strange thrill was making his blood course through his veins. He felt alive and excited and confident that he could take on this piece of tumbleweed, or anyone else for that matter, who challenged him. He flexed his fingers again, sending some men scrabbling for cover behind the bar, chairs and tables.

'C'mon, stranger,' he said mockingly. 'You don't need to — '

Jake never got to finish his sentence because that was when Ike thought he'd take his chance. His arm dropped to his side, his fingers reaching for the butt of his pistol.

When asked later, even the men closest to the gunfighters never saw what happened. One minute the stranger was unarmed, the next his pearl-handled Colt .45 had leapt into his hand and dispatched two slugs into the boy's chest before Ike's gun had even left his holster.

Jake watched as the boy slowly sank to his knees, a patch of deep red beginning to flower and spread across his chest. A look of surprise etched across his boyish face as Ike keeled over and lay motionless, face down in the grey sawdust on the bar room floor.

There was a few seconds pause before the saloon erupted into chaos. As men rushed forward to see the dead body, a couple of his buddies were already beginning to lift him off the floor.

'Get the doc!' someone shouted, even though they knew it would be a waste of time. It was the undertaker who was needed.

Jake quietly moved back into the crowd and disappeared out of the batwing doors, into the cool, starlit night before anyone realized he had gone.

Within fifteen minutes of the boy departing this earth, Jake Chalmers had saddled up and was galloping out of town with blood on his hands and another man's face to trouble his sleep.

2

By the time Jake had passed the weathered sign that declared 'Welcome To Sweetwater', the New Mexico sun had just about finished its punishing business for the day.

He pulled gently on Paulo's reins and the palomino obediently slowed to a halt in the dusty shale. Jake thoughtfully surveyed the town lying spread below him. He swept off his black Stetson and wiped the back of his neck with a neckerchief that used to be light blue before sweat and trail dust dyed it gray. Pushing a mop of dark hair away from his lean, tanned face, he took a slow pull out of his canteen and turned stiffly in the saddle to survey the foothills he had just left.

It had taken him five hard days before he was satisfied he was not being followed by anyone from Winters

Creek. Five hot days and five freezing nights since he had galloped out of town, keeping to little-known Indian tracks and dried river beds to cover his trail. He dared not light a fire at night, so he shivered as the temperature plummeted, keeping himself as warm as he could wrapped in a single woollen blanket and the old tarp he kept rolled on the back of his saddle.

He slept little. Even when sleep did come it brought little comfort. Despite the bitter cold he often woke in a feverish, dripping sweat. Since he had been fourteen, Jake could hardly remember a night when the same bad dreams hadn't disturbed him. With a shake of his mane Paulo snickered and woke Jake from his memories.

'Whoa, boy, steady,' he said and smiled as he rubbed the pony's neck. Jake suddenly felt pangs of hunger stab his belly. Dried pemmican biscuits and salted beef jerky were enough to keep a man from dying from hunger but after a while, they were pretty lean pickings.

He stared at the town shimmering in the dying heat of the day. It had been a few years since he'd last been to Sweetwater. Near the border of Texas and close to the Pecos River, it was plumb on the Goodnight-Loving trail and was a welcome stop for the thousands of steers and their cowhands as they made their way to the railheads at Pueblo, Denver or Cheyenne. To the east of the growing main street he could just make out the corrals, filled with milling steers ready to be herded out on the next stage of their drive.

He remembered it as small enough to be friendly but big enough for a stranger's face to go unnoticed for a while: just the sort of place he needed right now. But, looking down at it now, he could see that it had grown quite a bit since last he'd been here. Like so many other small towns in the West, Sweetwater had thrived and prospered with the influx of cattle, but Jake knew that with all that money came greed and where there was greed, trouble wasn't far behind.

For a moment, he thought about skirting the town altogether but the long drag he had taken out of his canteen changed his mind. Spitting out the brackish fluid into the dust, he decided that some sweet water was exactly what they both needed.

He wasn't sure what his plans would be exactly but he reckoned they could rest up here for a few days before moving on. By then he would know whether there was anyone on his tail and then he could carry on his zigzag journey through Texas and across the Rio Grande into Mexico. There, he thought, he'd be safe enough from anybody who might be wanting to talk to him regarding the gunfight in Winters Creek. He reached down and gently rubbed Paulo's ears.

'Well, boy, nothing else for it. I reckon we'll go down there and take our chances. Just don't you go doing something I'll regret.'

Paulo snickered and nodded his head

as if in agreement, shaking his long blond mane. Jake allowed himself a wry smile as he gave Paulo's sides a gentle squeeze with his spurs and urged him down the hill towards Sweetwater and whatever lay in store for them.

3

Less than half an hour later, Jake had entered Sweetwater's main street.

It was bustling with buggies and buckboards, cowboys on horseback and townsfolk busily going about their business up and down the wide, dusty thoroughfare.

He knew the place would have changed but he couldn't have guessed by how much. It seemed that the town couldn't grow quickly enough to cater for the swell of people riding on the back of the booming cattle trade. This, in turn, was being driven by the insatiable demand for fresh beef in cities and towns on the East coast.

Everywhere you looked there was some sort of construction going on. The sound of hammering, sawing and men yelling instructions could be heard everywhere above the normal street noise. Old buildings were growing upwards, with new storeys being added, and outwards, with false fronts, sidewalks and porches. New buildings were going up at each end of the main street, almost doubling its length. As he passed, Jake counted at least ten saloons, three hotels, two eating-houses, a large general store, and he had no doubt there were more than a few parlour houses doing a thriving trade somewhere. Over the noise of the busy street, banjo and piano music and loud laughter billowed out of every saloon he passed. It wasn't even dusk yet.

Could get lively here of an evening, thought Jake.

There was still the same old church that doubled as the school hall — he guessed there wasn't much profit to be had in religion and learning in Sweetwater.

He passed the busy blacksmith's, who was also the local sign-maker and if the piles of newly painted boards propped up outside his workshop was anything to go by, new businesses must have been springing up everyday. Beside the blacksmith's was the barber, where a queue of rough-looking cattle-drivers was waiting outside for much-needed haircuts and shaves. Next in line was the undertaker, his stock of pine coffins lined up outside his place of business in a macabre display. He'd even put prices on them and business looked as though it was thriving, which gave Jake a sinking feeling in his gut.

The town had even got itself a newspaper. Across the glass-fronted office, large gold letters proudly declared that this was the home of the *Sweetwater Chronicle*. Through the dusty windows, he saw a small shirtsleeved gent with a black waistcoat and a bowler hat piling large sheets of white paper into a big machine the likes of which Jake had never seen. With loud mechanical clunks and hisses of steam that made it sound like a small locomotive, the machine was sliding out freshly printed pages. Yessir, Sweetwater was surely getting big ideas about itself.

Horses were lined up along the hitching rails and kids played noisily among them. A small dog barked excitedly around their hoofs. As he made his way along the street he caught his reflection in a store window. If it were not for his straight, upright bearing he could have been taken for a drifting saddle bum. His leather boots and chaps were filthy and scuffed. His black pants, blue shirt and vest were dusted with the orange hue of the mountains. Hard stubble made a dark shadow around his strong chin and the rim of his Stetson was battered and uneven. The only thing that looked untainted by the rigours of his journey was his Colt .45, reflecting the painstaking care and attention it received every night.

Jake rubbed his chin ruefully. As he passed Sweetwater's new hotels and saloons, his body ached for a hot bath, close shave and some clean clothes, but he had to fix Paulo first. What he really needed was a livery stable. Once Paulo was rubbed down, watered and fed, he would see to his own needs.

On the sidewalk, outside what looked like a thriving real estate office, a Mexican was lounging on an old creaking rocking chair, smoking a roll-up, enjoying the temperature going down. His wide brimmed hat was tilted forward, covering most of his face. Jake halted Paulo in front of him and loudly cleared his throat.

'Pardon me,' he said.

The Mexican cowboy didn't move at first, then, lazily, he pushed his hat back to the top of his head. Black, suspicious eyes looked Jake up and down. He didn't say anything but spat on the sidewalk.

'I'm looking for a livery. Need to get my horse bedded down for the night.'

The Mexican removed the smoking cigarette from his mouth.

'So?' he said in an arrogant drawl.

Jake felt his hackles rise but held his tongue. He'd just got away from one piece of trouble. He didn't intend in riding straight into another.

'If you could point me in the right direction, I'd be much obliged.'

Eventually the Mexican nodded towards the corrals at the end of the street.

'Abe McDonnel's place. Bed and board. Buy or hire. Can't miss it,' he drawled.

He then pushed back on the chair and pulled his hat forward. The conversation was over. This particular inhabitant of Sweetwater had done all the good citizenship he was going to do for the day.

'Much obliged,' murmured Jake, tipping the edge of his Stetson. He turned to follow the man's rough directions.

A few hundred yards later he spotted a large barn with big weathered white letters painted on the side. Next to the barn were a couple of lean-tos and, out front, a small corral, divided into pens. Four black geldings and some mules were tethered there, ignoring the dozen or so chickens busily pecking and scratching at the baked soil around their legs.

As Jake stiffly dismounted in the yard a small, balding man shuffled out through the barn doors. His face was haggard with silvery grey stubble and watery eyes. He limped badly. His once red shirt was faded and holed at the sleeves and his suspenders hung loosely from his grubby breeches. A clay pipe hung from the side of his toothless mouth. As he limped towards Jake he eyed him suspiciously, lingering just a fraction too long on the shining Colt strapped to his leg.

'Abe McDonnell,' he said, by way of introduction. 'Can I help you?'

'Like to book this fellah in for two, maybe three days.'

'What is it? Two or three?'

'Depends.'

'Depends on what?'

Jake stared at the old man.

'It depends,' he said slowly, 'on how long I decide to stay.'

The old man took the pipe out of his mouth and blue smoke leaked between his lips. He spat in the dust.

'Here on business, mister?'

'Maybe.'

'You come far?'

He looked past Jake to Paulo who was impatiently snorting and pawing the ground, shaking his head irritably. He trembled slightly and flecks of foam were still on his flanks and muzzle.

'I've come far enough.'

'Where ya headin'?' enquired the old man.

Jake narrowed his eyes and stared hard at him.

'You know,' murmured Jake, 'you ask a lot of questions. I just want my horse bedded down and looked after. Now it seems you don't need to know a whole lot more than that. If you don't want my money, I'll find someone else who does.'

Jake started to turn away, gathering Paulo's reins. The old man spat again.

'Now don't go gettin' yoursel' into a

lather, boy,' protested Abe, 'I jist likes to know who I'm dealin' with. Things ain't what they used to be around these parts.'

Jake stopped.

'All right, all right,' said Abe, 'take him over to the barn.'

That was when Jake saw her. She must have come out of the barn when he was talking to the old man. She was slim, no more than twenty-one, her hair was so golden, if Jake had been a prospector he'd have put a claim on it.

She wore a red-checked shirt and a dark split riding-skirt that failed to conceal the curves hidden below. Leaning casually on the corral, a riding-boot on the bottom rung, she rested her chin on her folded arms and looked thoughtfully in their direction, although whether it was the old man, Paulo or himself she was most interested in was difficult for Jake to tell.

The old man's rough voice cut through Jake's reverie.

'Elaine? Deal with this gent's horse, will ya?'

Jake wondered what Elaine was to this old man. Surely not his wife. His daughter maybe?

'Git your saddles and any other gear you need and the girl will show you where to stow it. She'll take good care of your beast all right.'

She walked towards them and took Paulo's reins, stroking his muzzle and speaking softly into his ears, but she ignored his rider. For the first time in his life, Jake was envious of a horse.

Elaine gently led Paulo into the cool, dark inside of the barn. As she tethered him up in a clean stall Jake deftly undid the girth strap and removed his saddle and saddle-bags.

'They'll be safe here,' she said eventually, not hostile but definitely not friendly either.

Jake swung his saddle over the wooden partition and, though there was no reason to remain, he found he didn't want to go. He found himself wishing she would ask as many questions as her father. He would have been far more willing to get involved in conversation with her.

Finding a loose piece of straw, he nibbled it thoughtfully as he watched her work. She lifted half a sack of grain with surprising ease and arranged it close to Paulo, who nudged the sack open and started munching contentedly. Once she had poured a bucket of clean water into the trough, she picked up two stiff brushes and started working on Paulo's flanks with long, firm but gentle strokes.

She looked up and caught him watching her intently. She returned his gaze.

'He'll need a new shoe. Front left,' she said.

'How can you tell?' asked Jake, 'you ain't even lifted his leg.'

'It's my job to tell. I think you've been riding him too hard over the hills.'

'Who says I came over the hills?'

'The marks on his hoofs. The state you're in. The horse is cleaner. Smells better too, I reckon.'

Jake smiled.

'We've been on the move a while,' he admitted.

For the first time that he could remember, he found himself wanting to talk. He knew he was ignoring his personal rules on never getting close to anybody, never carrying excess baggage, never picking up anything he wouldn't be afraid to drop when it came time to run again. These were the strict, self-imposed laws he lived by and they had saved his life many times.

'You'll need to rest him before you move on. Build up his strength.'

'I might be around a while.'

She raised her eyebrows.

'Really? What are you? A hired gun? You working for Jordan Carter?'

Jake narrowed his eyes defensively.

'I don't work for anyone — especially someone I've never heard of before. Who's Jordan Carter?'

She started to brush the horse a little more fiercely.

'Well, he'll have heard of you before

long — probably knows you're in town right now. Nothing gets past him for long. We've enough men like you in Sweetwater, Mr Chalmers, if that is your real name. You types drift in from nowhere, wearing your guns as though it makes you invincible. Then, when you've done your damage, given us a few more widows, left another couple of orphans, you ride straight back out again without a glance back. The busiest man since Jordan Carter came to this town is Hank Bellows, the undertaker.'

Her cheeks were now lightly flushed with anger.

'It'll be a pleasure to look after Paulo here but, Mr Chalmers, you're the last type of person we need here in Sweetwater!'

She slapped the two grooming-brushes together with a crack that made Paulo start, and threw them in a wooden box. She stood with her hands on her hips ready to say something else, then changed her mind before turning her back on him and disappearing up the barn and out into the backyard.

He was left numbed by her cold hostility, but unsettled because her words rang true. She didn't know him — how could she? — but she had just described the way he felt about himself.

Even after all these years, Jake had never got used to taking another man's life and he secretly prayed he never would. He wished that in this part of the world there was some other way for people to protect themselves. His pa had believed in another way but he had paid for that belief with his life and the life of his mother.

The only consolation, Jake told himself, was that he had never taken a man's life needlessly and always in self-defence. All his victims had looked him in the eye when they died but that was little comfort. Elaine's talk of widows and orphans made the weight in his heart grow a little heavier.

He watched her go, then patted Paulo's neck as he left.

'I'm sure she'll be nicer to you, pal.'

Out in the yard he passed Abe McDonnell sitting by the well, polishing a bridle, deep in concentration.

'Is that you sorted?' he said, looking up as Jake approached.

'The horse is getting taken care of, if that's what you mean?'

He watched the old man for a few moments then said, 'Your daughter seems to have a real sliver under her skin about me.'

'Nope! Not you exactly,' said Abe and spat in the dust. 'It's that pistol you're packin'. Hates 'em. Hates the folks that carry 'em. Especially those who know how to use 'em — like yourself,' he added.

Jake ignored that.

'How come?'

'A year ago now, her ma got caught with a stray slug from a couple of roisterers settling a gambling score in the street. So drunk they couldn't see each other. They walked away the best of buddies, and Elaine had lost her ma and I was a widower.'

Jake lowered his eyes to the toe of his scuffed boot. There was that cut in his heart again. 'I'm sorry to hear it. Didn't the sheriff do anything?'

Abe looked up sharply.

'Couldn't bring Mary back, could he?'

Jake shook his head.

'I guess not.'

Abe started cleaning the bridle again, now with a new vigour.

'Anyhow, Luke Gardner, our sheriff, he ain't the man he used to be.' He went silent, then bundled his cloth into his clenched fist. He looked up sharply at Jake. 'I told you, mister. Nothin' ain't what it used to be around here any more. Tell you the honest truth, I don't like gunslingers myself.'

He stood up and threw the bridle over his shoulder.

'Anyway, no point jawin' about it.'

Before Abe limped off, Jake dug into his saddle-bag slung over his shoulder and paid him one week's board in advance. He did this for three reasons.

One was that he didn't want to hang around to square him up if he had to leave town in a hurry. Secondly, he wanted Paulo well looked after and third; he hoped that Abe might just say a good word about him to Elaine.

4

After leaving the livery stable, Jake walked back on to the main street along the dried and warped boardwalks.

As he passed the sheriff's office the door swung open and a heavily built white-haired man came out into the daylight. He looked as though he was going somewhere on an errand, but when he noticed the scruffy stranger he stopped, pulled the door slowly behind him and hitched up his gun belt round his ample girth. Surveying Jake quickly from head to foot, he took in the stranger's face, build and, with more interest, the gleaming pearl-handled .45 that sat loosely in his holster. When he thought he had seen enough, he straightened his calfskin vest. The silver badge pinned to the lapel of his vest flashed in the sun.

Jake raised a hand to the rim of his

hat in acknowledgement and their eyes locked for a moment. The sheriff nodded slightly as Jake passed him and then stood for a while and watched the stranger until he was out of view. Jake could feel the sheriff's eyes burn in his back. He was left with the feeling that their paths would cross again; and soon.

As he walked along the main street, Jake began to realize that Sweetwater was no longer a town at peace with itself. People's lives were going on all around him and on the surface it was just another typical Western boom town, but so far all he had met with was distrust and suspicion.

He had felt it in the guarded welcome of Abe, the cold hostility of Elaine and now the almost fearful wariness of the sheriff. Jake decided there and then he wouldn't be staying as long as he had planned. Once he had washed, filled his belly and rested both himself and Paulo, he would be heading off at first light tomorrow.

A sign showing vacancies hung on

the window of the Alhambra Hotel and Jake checked in. It wasn't the biggest or the cheapest hostelry in town but it suited his purposes. The clerk inspected his name as he signed in at the desk.

'Staying long, Mr . . . er . . . Chalmers?' He beamed with a false, toothy grin.

'I'll let you know when I'm checking out.'

'Here on business?'

Jake put the pen down firmly on the reception desk's newly varnished surface. He peeled off the required number of greenbacks for one night's stay and laid them next to it.

'You've got my name. You've got my money. I reckon that's about all you need. Can I have my key to my room now?'

The clerk nodded eagerly, suddenly keen not to offend in a town where customers often complained with a gun in their hands. Jake followed him up the stairs to a small room at the end of the landing, which looked over the main street.

'Anything else, Mr Chalmers?' asked the clerk after he had let Jake into the sparsely furnished room.

'A hot bath and some good chow would be good.'

'Coming right up, Mr Chalmers,' said the clerk. He backed out of the door to hurry down the corridor and take up his place again at reception.

Two hours later, Jake had crossed the road to the Eldorado saloon and was sitting at a corner table sipping a cold beer. A hot bath, close shave and clean clothes made him look and feel a new man. His first hot meal for days: beefsteak, sweet potatoes and beans had gone down well and he was now looking forward to spending a few hours in the bar in his own company. He planned on a quiet night and hitting the hay early.

He'd thought about maybe heading down to the McDonnells' place to check on Paulo, although he hated to admit to himself that the real reason was that he hoped he would see Elaine again. Then he recalled the angry fire in her eyes and decided maybe he would leave it.

The Eldorado was a typical saloon for this part of the territory. A hazy blue pall of cigar smoke lingered in the air over the crowds of thirsty cowmen and punchers. In the corner a shirtsleeved pianist tried valiantly to make his honky-tonk piano heard above the raucous noise.

Half a dozen percentage girls in bright red, blue and green silk dresses were circulating, teasing and flirting. A couple of girls had approached Jake, sitting on his knees or taking his arm but he made it plain he wasn't open to their advances and they soon left him in peace.

Around him, there were a few games of blackjack and poker going on. He thought maybe he'd try parting some of these boys from the cash they all seemed so loose with. He was studying the poor hand of a guy who had his back to him when a shadow flitted on his blind side, blocking out the light.

Before he'd even turned around, Jake had gripped his Colt and had it cocked and pointed in the face of the intruder. Another few pounds of pressure on the slim trigger and the man now gazing down at him would have been left without a face.

The first thing he saw was the silver badge. The next thing he saw was the chubby face of Sheriff Gardner.

'You're mighty jumpy, son,' said the sheriff drawing on a slim roll-up that momentarily masked his face in a cloud of smoke and made him narrow his eyes.

'I don't like people creeping up on my blind side. Makes me nervous,' said Jake. He uncocked the Colt and let it fall gently into its resting-place on his hip.

'Nervous, eh? You got something to hide?'

'Everybody's got something to hide, Sheriff.'

The sheriff thought about this for a moment.

'Saw you ride into town this morning. You plan on staying long?'

'You know, Sheriff,' said Jake, turning round in his seat to look the older man full in the eyes, 'everybody I've met in this town seems mighty interested in my business. That's about the third time I've been asked that question today.'

'Well, your business is my business.'

Jake didn't comment. The sheriff pulled again on his cigarette.

'And going by the way you pulled that gun on me, I don't think Sweetwater wants your type of business. You're mighty quick, son. Either you're running from trouble or you're looking for it. Either way, I don't think we want you in Sweetwater.'

'I take it you're not the welcoming committee — '

'Now don't start gettin' sassy with me, boy, or I'll — '

'Trouble, Sheriff?'

Behind Luke Gardner stood a tall, slim man. His face was lean and dark-skinned and his white, straight teeth were topped with a black pencil-line moustache. Dressed in a black frock-coat, pinstripe trousers and frilled shirt with a bootlace tie, he looked as though he'd just got off a Mississippi riverboat.

Behind him stood a large bulky bruiser with a nose that had been broken a few times and beside him, a smaller, younger man than the gambler but with unmistakably similar features.

'I don't believe I've had the pleasure,' said the newcomer looking at Jake. 'Jordan Carter's the name. I own this place.'

He waved his arm to indicate the Eldorado but Jake didn't know if he meant the saloon in particular or the whole town in general. Jake shook the proffered hand. It was indeed the hand of a gambler. It was smooth and soft, a stranger to hard work but with the strength of flexible and supple fingers.

'Jake Chalmers' the name.'

'Pleased to meet you, Mr Chalmers.' He turned to the men standing beside him. 'This is Pete Grundy who works for me and this is my younger brother, Nate.' The two men didn't smile or offer their hands but merely grunted acknowledgment.

'I'm sorry for interrupting,' continued Jordan Carter. 'Were you two gentlemen discussing something?'

The sheriff's demeanour had changed. Jack sensed that he was afraid of Carter although he was sure he would have denied it with his dying breath.

'I was just telling Chalmers here that we don't like trouble here in Sweetwater.'

'Mmmm. You're right, of course, Sheriff,' said Carter, thoughtfully smoothing his moustache with his thumb and forefinger. 'I hope you don't mind me remarking, Mr Chalmers, but I couldn't help but notice the way you handled that gun. You're pretty quick. Do you use that thing . . . professionally?'

Before Jake could reply the sheriff cut in.

'I don't think we need any more professional gunslingers in this town — '

Carter held up his hand, silencing the older man.

'Sheriff Gardner, whom I choose to hire is no one's concern but mine.'

'There's already a small army of hired guns working for you — '

'*Employees*, Sheriff, *employees*. There've been a few occasions when you've been grateful for their assistance, have you not?'

The sheriff reddened a little. 'That might be true but . . . ' His words petered out; he was quickly out of his depth with this cool hustler. The two men stared at each other in venomous silence.

Jake cleared his throat.

'I hate to interrupt you two gentlemen, but since this conversation is about me, let me save you some of your breath. I only use this gun when I need to and I don't work for anyone.' He looked up at the sheriff. 'I also don't like being shoved around. I go where I choose when I choose and if you've got a problem with that you can show me the law that says I can't. So if you two gentlemen would like to continue your conversation elsewhere then I can get on with my beer in peace.'

Carter was not used to being spoken to like this, especially in his own bar, but a poker-player of his experience knew how to hide his true feelings. Masking his anger, he smiled broadly.

'Well, you seem to have set the record straight there, Mr Chalmers. I hope you enjoy your *brief* stay.'

Jake didn't miss the emphasis on the word 'brief'. Then, with a small nod to the two men, Jordan Carter walked back to the bar, his two henchmen trailing behind him like a pair of loyal gun dogs.

Jake and the sheriff watched them go until they were out of hearing.

'Seems Mr Carter carries a lot of weight around here,' said Jake.

'Yeah, he owns a few businesses and gets rent from half the others in

Sweetwater. Got big plans for the future, too. Aims to run for mayor in the next election and, one way or another, he'll probably win it too. Who's gonna stand against him? No sir, you don't want to get on the wrong side of Mr Jordan Carter,' said Luke.

'They used to say that about the law,' murmured Jake.

Gardner threw his cigarette end on the floor in exasperation and roughly stamped on it.

'Listen, Mister. Jordan Carter is the law in Sweetwater and there's not a lot I can do about it neither. Come election time and he gets in, he'll soon be looking to even the score with anyone damn fool enough to get in his way.'

'I'm surprised he's even bothering with an election if he's got all the firepower you say he has.'

A grim smile spread on the older man's face.

'He's in a hurry, but he's no fool. He knows he needs to keep just on the right side on the law so that . . . '

Suddenly the sheriff stopped. He didn't know this stranger from Adam and here he was blabbing his mouth off in one of Carter's places.

'Anyway, that's none of my business and if you want to keep your head you'll not make it any of yours either. Just stay out of trouble. Remember that!'

The lawman turned and stomped out of the saloon, pushing the batwing doors furiously as he left.

Jake rocked back on the legs of his chair, took a swig of beer and thought about the two men he had just met. There was no doubt Carter was a big-time crook and the sheriff was in his pocket, although deep down in the old man Jake saw the last burning embers of pride in that old tin badge he wore. Anyway, it was none of his business. He decided he would be staying well out of the way of both of them. With that thought Jake finished his beer in one mouthful and left the saloon for the night.

5

Jake made his way across the street in the darkness to the Alhambra Hotel. Once in his room, he made sure the door was securely locked before sitting on the edge of his bed. With an effort he pulled off his boots. He doused the kerosene lamp till the wick was just a blue dot, then lay back on the soft mattress and closed his eyes. But, as usual, sleep didn't come. The bed was too soft, the room was too warm and his mind kept going over the people he had met since arriving in Sweetwater: Luke Gardner, Jordan Carter and, most frequently, Elaine McDonnell.

As the night wore on, the noisy drinking and revelling of the cowhands spilt into the street. There was hollering and shouting and every now and again the sound of bottles and glasses being broken. Arguments and small scuffles broke out and Jake knew it was only a matter of time before someone got badly hurt.

The next thing he knew he was on the floor scrabbling for his gun belt which he had draped over the chair beside his bed. A bullet had smashed through his window, scattering glass over the floorboards. He crawled to the window ledge and cautiously looked over.

Now there was lots of gunfire. Cowboys were letting off weapons in every direction. Horses were being raced up and down the street to yelps and whoops from a bunch of onlookers. Groups of men were in the street, drinking whiskey straight out of the bottles. It was mayhem.

Where is that damn sheriff when you need him? thought Jake.

He watched for a while but when the ruckus showed no sign of abating, Jake resigned himself to a night on the hard floorboards, under the window ledge, where a stray bullet couldn't reach him.

He was about to pull a blanket from the bed when he noticed that something had attracted the attention of the men to the north side of the town. They were whooping and hollering and shouting excitedly. Jake put his cheek on to the cool glass and looked in that direction.

A couple of drunken cowboys on horseback had grabbed the reins of a horse pulling a small black buggy and were guiding — almost dragging — the horse towards the centre of town. Jake heard a woman scream. As it came closer and stopped in front of the brightly lit saloon more of the revellers jumped into it. Two of them hauled the driver out into the dust.

He recognized Elaine McDonnell at once. She was fighting and kicking like a wildcat but that only served to amuse the cowhands more. With a groan, Jake knew what he had to do. Hurriedly, he shoved on his boots and was still strapping on his gunbelt as he ran down the stairs, then walked out on to the boardwalk. He stopped and leaned against the porch support, halfway in the shadows.

No one in the street noticed Jake arrive. The mob were too busy arguing about who would get first turn at the girl. One of them, a bearded, burly giant of a man had wrapped his arms completely around her in a crushing bear hug and her resistance was dwindling. Another one was in front of her, trying to force his face to her lips. She jerked her head from side to side frantically.

The single shot fired into the sand brought everyone to a standstill. Then one by one they turned round to Jake, who was slowly putting his gun back into his holster. For a moment a few of them wondered whether the shot had come from him at all.

'I don't think the lady is enjoying the party, gents,' said Jake.

At first they were all too stunned to think. Then the bear let Elaine drop to the ground as though she was a sack of grain. She lay there motionless. Her captor looked at Jake with a grim smile on his cruel lips.

'I don't know who you are, mister,' he growled, 'but you'd better have a good reason for interrupting our fun.'

'She didn't look as though she was having fun.'

'She was just about to.' He laughed crudely, although he never took his eyes from the stranger half-hidden in the shadows. He narrowed his eyes to see him better.

'I've got things to be gettin' on with, so I'm going to do you a great big favour. I'm going to forget you tried to break up our little old party here. I'm going to let you crawl back under the stone you came out of and me and my friends are going to get back to what we were doing. OK?'

Jake shook his head slowly.

' 'Fraid not. But I'll return the favour. You let her go and I'll let you live. Is that a deal?'

The men standing around looked nervously at each other. There was something in the cool, almost casual bearing of this stranger in the dark that made them feel sure this was not an empty bluff. He was either very foolish or very brave and he didn't look like a fool. The street had now gone very quiet and a crowd had spilled out of the Eldorado to watch the events unfold.

For an age it seemed the two men stood facing each other. Eventually the big man spoke.

'Come out where I can see you. I like to see a man's face before I kill him.'

Jake didn't move.

'There's no need for this. Just let the girl go and we'll all go home.'

Out of the side of his eye Jake saw a shadow move on the edge of the sidewalk. Without moving his head, he managed to see enough to recognize a large, burly figure. On his chest glinted a silver badge.

'Are you coming out to face me,' screamed the big man, 'or do I have to come in there and drag you out like the yellow-livered coyote you are?'

Jake walked slowly out of the shadow and down the two wooden steps on to the dust of the street. Not twelve feet separated the two men. Jake stood with his arms folded. His opponent spread his legs, his arms arched over his side, flexing his fingers hovering an inch above the two guns strapped to his side.

'After three, stranger,' he hissed.

Jake shook his head from side to side.

'One.'

The crowd as one took a step back.

'Two!'

Everyone braced themselves for the third number but it never came. The big man went for his guns, lurching forward, bending his knees but the guns never cleared his holster. He was already reeling backward, a howl of pain caught in his throat, a red splash of blood spreading across his broad, barrel chest. To his right, one of his cronies raised a rifle to avenge his partner. It spat a lick of fire but the slug buried itself into the ground not five feet ahead of him as he too fell backwards and lay, feet splayed in the sand. He lashed out one last kick, then lay still.

All this happened in seconds and when it was over, Jake stood motionless, his gun balanced loosely in his hand, the only movement the softly pirouetting blue smoke that leaked from the barrel of his Colt.

Time froze. Jakes eyes scanned the onlookers, waiting for any of them to make a move. And everyone knew it, so no one did. They had seen for themselves how deadly that gun had been.

Then things started happening. From nowhere, Abe McDonnell pushed his way through the crowd and let out a grief-stricken cry when he saw Elaine lying in the ground with the other two bodies.

'Oh, no, Lord — no, not again!'

He ran over, fell to his knees and cradled Elaine in his arms. Tears began to stream down his rough cheeks but they turned to tears of relief when Elaine opened her eyes and slowly, in a daze, rose to her feet. Leaning heavily on her pa, they turned towards the livery stable, the mob parting silently as they passed.

Almost at the same time, the crowd of men that had blocked the entrance to the Eldorado dispersed as Jordan Carter came strolling out on to the sidewalk. He came to the top step and thrust his thumbs deep into his velvet waistcoat. His voice carried clearly across the street.

'Well, well, Mr Chalmers. It seems you didn't heed my advice. You've had a busy night.' He surveyed the two bodies lying in the dust. 'I thought we'd made it clear we didn't want your kind of trouble. I don't know where you come from but in these parts, the cold-blooded gunning down of two innocent citizens is a hanging offence.'

'It was self-defence,' said Jake. 'They pulled on me first. I've got plenty of witnesses.'

'And who would they be?' said Carter with a smirk.

'All around you. These men here.'

Carter laughed.

'I think, Mr Chalmers, you'll have a problem finding anybody who would stand up in court to defend you.'

'I'll take my chances, Carter.'

Jordan Carter slowly walked down the steps and crossed the street to face Jake.

'Just in case you didn't realize earlier on, Chalmers, I'm the law around here. I'm judge and jury all rolled into one and I dispense my kind of justice quickly. Get him, boys!'

6

Jake winced with pain as the cold steel of a rifle barrel was pushed roughly into the back of his neck. He felt a sickening feeling in the pit of his stomach as he heard the mechanical click of the chamber being cocked. His gun was grabbed out of his hand. Jordan Carter looked on, a wry smile of amusement stretched across his mouth.

'Anyone gotta rope handy?' he smirked.

The crowd of men burst into life. They milled around, shouting and shoving until a rope was removed from the pommel of a nearby bronco and was thrown towards the self-appointed vigilante committee. It landed in the dust at Jake's feet.

His hands were pulled behind his back and expertly tied as tight as a steer ready for branding. A young cowboy, so drunk he could hardly stand, swiftly twisted the rope and presented a perfect hanging noose to the mob. It was roughly thrown over Jake's head and the thick rope came to lie on his shoulders. Suddenly, the noose was jerked tight and his head was thrown viciously to the side. He let out a low groan. The rope gouged at his throat and he felt his skin rubbed raw and red. There had been very few moments in Jake's life when he had tasted the bitter taste of fear but this was one of those moments.

The next thing he knew, two men had grabbed him from either side and dragged him to where a nearby oak tree provided the gallows the men needed. The rope was thrown over one of the lower branches and hauled tight so that Jake had to stand on the toes of his boots to keep contact with the ground.

Painfully, he somehow managed to turn his head to see Jordan Carter overseeing the lynch mob. Carter seemed detached from the whole thing as though Jake was just some dumb animal ready for slaughter. All the men's eyes were on him — waiting for the nod, the signal that would push Jake into oblivion. But Carter seemed in no hurry. He took a long, slow draw on his cheroot and lazily blew a cloud of blue smoke into the night. The night was cool. The men were quiet. He gazed up at the stars for what seemed to Jake an eternity. Then he looked around him.

'OK, boys,' he said eventually. 'Let's get this over with.'

Six men formed a team along the rope and took the strain. A surge of energy seemed to pass through the crowd of men who, with lots of pushing and jostling, formed a ragged semicircle around Jake. Few of them of their own accord would have considered themselves capable of cold-blooded murder and even fewer, in the cold light of day, would have thought they could have been party to this kind of 'justice'. But they were part of a frenzied hunting pack and the men's eyes were wild and filled with blood-lust.

The men on the rope took the strain. All they had to do now was to take half a dozen steps backward and Jake would be hoisted completely off the ground. It seemed that nothing was going to stop them finishing off their night's work — except the sound of a Winchester rifle being fired into the starlit sky.

'Let 'im go!'

The deep voice carried across the street and seemed to fill the street. For the second time that night, the men froze where they stood and a strange stillness descended on them as they searched around looking for the man who had uttered the words.

'I said, let 'im go!'

As the second shot passed close above their heads with a deadly whine, the men who held the rope let it fall into the sand and the strong hands that held Jake's arms let him go as though he was on fire.

'Now, anyone who tries to harm that boy gets the next bullet in his head!'

And this time, there was no doubt where the voice came from. Sheriff Gardner stood on the porch where Jake had stood just minutes before. A Winchester rifle was raised to his eye as he slowly scanned the crowd through the sight. Everyone knew the man — at least everyone recognized his face — but what was unfamiliar was the steely determination in his voice and the authority in his actions that left no doubt in anyone's minds that he meant just what he said.

'Luke? Is that you?' Carter shouted. He walked down the steps into the street, peered at the sheriff through the dark as though he could not believe his eyes. 'What in hell's name d'ye think you're doin'?'

'I'm doing my duty, Carter. There'll be no lynching this night on my watch.'

'But this is your duty.' Carter pointed angrily at Jake. 'This man is a murderer. He gunned down two of my men in cold blood. Right here in this street. In front of every man here. We demand justice!'

He spread his arm to encompass the mob who, emboldened by Carter's stance, murmured their agreement.

The sheriff shook his head stubbornly.

'Not the way I saw it. Not from where I was standing — and while I'm still wearing this badge, Carter, the law will go through its due process. I've closed my eyes to lots of things around here, but from now on, I'm playing it by the book. I'm placing this man under arrest until the next sitting of the circuit-riding judge. He's in my custody and any man who says different will just have to accept the consequences.'

Carter stared angrily at him.

'You're an old fool, Gardner. It'll be your word against this whole town. Not another body'll testify with you.'

Luke knew Carter was right and without at least another witness to defend Jake the outcome of the case was already decided. In truth, he probably would have been better just to let the hanging go ahead, as the outcome would be the same. Both men scanned the gathering for supporters. The crowd shuffled their feet uneasily and looked away, avoiding either man's eyes but for different reasons. They were frightened to look into Carter's and most were ashamed to look in the sheriff's.

Carter started to relax. He knew that not another man would defy him. If he had anything to do with it, Jake would swing tonight and then, when the time was right, he would sort out this meddlesome old man. He'd served his purpose, he'd tolerated him too long already. Carter smiled and visibly relaxed.

'Looks like it's you against the whole town, old man,' he sneered and started to turn around to give the order for the men to carry on with Jake's execution. Another voice made him stop.

'The sheriff's right. I saw it too!'

Neville Chuster, proprietor and editor of the *Sweetwater Chronicle*, emerged out of the shadows and made his way to stand alongside the sheriff. Gold-wire spectacles clung to the end of his nose but behind that glass shone bright, intelligent and determined eyes.

'Thank you, Neville,' Gardner almost whispered. He cocked the rifle hard and raised his voice. 'Now, I'm getting tired of repeating myself, but I'll say it just one more time. Let that man go.'

Carter stared narrow-eyed at the two men on the boardwalk. He weighed his options and wondered whether to finish this thing tonight once and for all and just string these two troublemakers up alongside Jake. But no, he didn't want to rush things. Not when he'd worked so hard to get control of the town. He'd get even with the sheriff and the newsman but not yet. Not tonight.

He nodded to the two thugs who still stood on either side of Jake. The noose was slackened and lifted over his head and there was a flash of a knife as the rope that bound his hands were sliced apart. With no one to support him, Jake slowly slipped to his knees. He rubbed the burns around his neck while trying to suck clean air into his lungs.

'Go help him, Neville. I'll cover you,' said Luke quietly.

Neville jumped from the boardwalk into the street and ran across to where Jake was still on his knees, coughing and spluttering in the dust. He reached down and swung Jake's arm around his shoulders. With an arm around his waist he pulled Jake to his feet.

'Can you walk?' whispered Neville into his ear.

Jake tried to speak but no sound came. Instead, he gave a brief nod of his head.

'Then let's get out of here,' muttered Neville.

'Wait . . . ' hissed Jake although Neville could barely make out the word.

'What is it, Jake?'

'My gun . . . '

Neville looked over his shoulder.

'Where's this man's gun?' he shouted at the crowd.

Someone handed him Jake's ivory-handled Colt and he stuffed it into his belt. Then slowly, uncertainly, the gunslinger and the newsman crossed the street and up the boardwalk to the sheriff.

'Make your way to the jailhouse,' said Gardner in a low voice.

As Jake and Neville shuffled along the boardwalk, the sheriff followed behind, walking backwards to cover the two men, never once taking his sights off the crowd of men who watched their every move. They shuffled restlessly and rumbled their disapproval but no one moved.

'You're making a big mistake, Sheriff,' shouted Carter. He spat out his smoked-down cheroot and ground the butt into the dust with the heel of a black boot, then angrily swung round. Ignoring the men around him he stormed back through the saloon's batwing doors, which banged loudly after him.

Not one of the men left standing in the street who watched them go would have traded places with Luke, Neville or Jake for a million dollars.

7

With Luke covering their backs, Neville half-carried, half-dragged Jake along the darkened boardwalk. After what seemed an age they reached the sheriff's office and almost fell through the doorway into the dark interior. As soon as they were safely inside, Luke bolted the door behind them and hastily pulled the dark-green window shades down.

'Stay away from the windows,' Luke murmured to Neville as he helped him lower Jake carefully into the sheriff's leather chair. Jake's head lolled back and he let out a muffled groan. Neville stared at the nasty, livid streak where the rope had burned a circle.

'I think we'll need the doc to have a look at that,' said Luke, as he turned up the large kerosene lamp on his desk, 'but first, I think we all need a little dose of another kind of medicine.'

As the pale-yellow light filled the spartan office he reached into the bottom desk-drawer, lifted out a bottle of whiskey and three small glasses. He filled them two fingers deep and handed them round. None of the men said a word until they had dispatched the dark-gold liquid in one eager gulp. The whiskey burned comfortingly and although Neville broke into a bout of coughing, he didn't refuse a refill.

It had started to slowly dawn on the three men just how close they had come to losing their lives. They were also realizing that far from being the end of the matter, this was just the beginning. They knew Carter would not allow his public humiliation to go unpunished.

'You didn't have to get involved you know,' said the old sheriff eventually, breaking the heavy silence. Neville removed his gold-framed spectacles and rubbed his eyes.

'I know I didn't, but I couldn't just stand back and let Carter walk all over you like that. When I saw you taking a stand . . . well, it didn't seem fair for you to shoulder it all on your own.'

'Thanks, Neville. I guess I owe you. I just wish there were a few more like you in Sweetwater. Then Carter couldn't keep getting away with riding roughshod over everybody in this town.'

Luke glanced across at the young man slumped in his chair. Jake was staring into the bottom of his empty glass.

'What are you going to do now, Jake?'

Jake looked up and gave the two men a grim smile.

'I'm not going anywhere, am I? I guess I'm under arrest,' he managed to say.

Luke rubbed the bridge of his nose and began to refill everyone's glasses.

'Nope, you're free to go. If you want to ride out of here tonight and never look back, well, that's up to you.'

'And what will you two do?'

Luke shrugged.

'To be honest, I don't know. We can't

hide in here for ever. The only thing I do know for certain is that my days as sheriff are numbered. One way or the other, Carter will see to it. He'll either remove me after his rigged elections or, more likely, there'll be a bullet waiting for me one dark night when I'm doing my rounds. That's the way he works.'

The sheriff put the bottle back into the bottom drawer and slammed the door shut.

'No sir, you don't cross Jordan Carter the way we did tonight and live to tell the tale for long.'

Jake turned to Neville.

'And what about you?'

Neville pushed his round spectacles up on to his nose and sighed deeply.

'I ain't going nowhere. Nowhere for me to go. Everything I own is in that newspaper office.'

Neville sat down on the edge of the desk, suddenly looking weary and older.

'I used to write for a big paper out East. They sent me out here three years ago for a story on the beef bonanza and

I never went back. When my pa died and left me some money, I set up the *Chronicle.*' He scratched his chin and laughed grimly. 'I was a lot younger and greener then. I saw myself as the voice of truth and justice in these parts. I thought my pen was mightier than the sword. I guess I was wrong. Seems the only truth around here is what comes out of the end of a gun.'

'Carter ain't going to let you get away with what you did tonight, you know that?' said Luke.

'I'm getting used to it,' said Neville, 'Carter's been trying to get control of my paper for a couple of years now. He's threatened a few times to shut me down if I print anything against him but I've managed to hold out so far.'

'Tell me about Carter,' said Jake thoughtfully.

Neville sat forward eagerly. Out of place and out of his depth where gunplay was concerned, he now looked every bit the newspaperman.

'Well, Carter came to Sweetwater

about five years ago.' He looked across at Luke and Luke nodded in agreement.

'He arrived with a pile of money. No one knows how he made it but you can bet it wasn't with honest sweat. Anyway, he came here buying up this and that. First a saloon, then a hotel, then a cathouse. Now, he owns about half the town and he's got some sort of stake in the other half. No one buys or sells a needle around here without Carter getting a cut somewhere in the deal. You can say what you like about his morals, but he's sharp as a tack when it comes to spotting a business opportunity. When the cattle drives started a few years back, he saw the money to be made. He's even got deals supplying Fort Smith and the Indian reservation with beeves. Yessir, Jordan Carter's been real smart. And it's not been all bad news. No sir, not by a long chalk. A lot of people in the town have made a lot of money on the back of the boom in Sweetwater — but that's only because it suits Carter. I truly think he's just biding his time until he and his private army take over everything and squeezes this place dry.'

'How's he going to do that?' asked Jake.

'A rumour that's going around is that he's planning on staking a claim for mining gold in the hills.'

'There's gold? Here in Sweetwater?' asked Jake in disbelief.

Neville shook his head.

'Not a dime's worth, otherwise it would have been found by now. No, there's no money in gold in these parts — but there is in selling supplies to goldminers who come here to try and find it. He can easily get a fraudulent sample made up to prove it. Word will soon spread. In fact, knowing the way Carter works, he'd look as though he was trying hard to hide it and within days there would be enough prospectors and miners to set up another town the size of Sweetwater. Hungry and thirsty men who'll need grub, stores, whiskey and women. And who is in the best position to supply it?'

'Carter.' Jake nodded with reluctant admiration. He had to admit the plan would work. Jordan Carter would wind up a very rich man even if not one nugget of gold was found.

Luke sat on the edge of the desk and stared down at Jake.

'But in the wake of the gold rush all that would remain would be a broken town. All the decent folk would move out, leaving everything behind without a dime to show for all their hard work. Within six months, Sweetwater would be a ghost town.'

'Surely somebody can stop him?' said Jake.

Luke shook his head.

'You've seen him in action. He's surrounded himself with a team of fast guns. That was his brother Nate you saw earlier on in the saloon. They look alike but that's where the likeness ends. Sure, they've both got a ruthless streak about a mile wide but Carter's a real cool customer whereas Nate's temper is on a hair-trigger. Fancies himself as a big-time gunslinger — and no one's going to challenge him as long as he is hiding behind his big brother.'

'The Carters are untouchable,' agreed Neville. 'Seems like he's the only law we have around here . . . '

Neville's voice trailed off as he realized what he had just said.

'I'm sorry, Luke . . . I didn't mean . . . '

Luke glanced up quickly then smiled.

'No offence taken, Neville. After all, it's the truth. Guess I'm not as young as I used to be.' He sighed heavily. 'When Carter came along, like a fool, I thought we could help each other out. Carter promised he'd keep me on — even give me a pension and a small homestead to retire to — as long as I didn't meddle too closely in his affairs. He supplied the muscle to keep the town in order, and for a while it was working out OK. But tonight, when I saw what was happening to young

Elaine, I knew I had let it get way out of hand. I knew I couldn't let it go on.' Luke looked at Jake. 'You were more of a lawman tonight than I've ever been.'

Jake smiled. 'I don't think you've anything to be ashamed about, Luke. Most men would have done the same things in your boots.'

'Not you, though.'

'Maybe. Maybe not.'

'So what are you gonna do, Jake?' asked Nevillle.

Jake got up and wandered to the window. He pulled the blinds slightly to one side. The street was empty and quiet. At least for tonight, the citizens of Sweetwater could sleep soundly, the way they should always be able to.

He turned to face the two men sitting glumly staring at the wooden floor but when he spoke, it was as though he was speaking to himself.

'Sometimes it seems I've spent my whole life running away. Tonight just might be the time to stop.'

8

The early-morning sun leaked through the small barred window and shone on Jake's face. His eyes flickered open and he lay for a moment trying to get his fuzzy head together.

Blinking in the harsh light, he looked around him, then sat up quickly and swung his legs over the low bunk, trying to remember how he had got himself locked up in a cell. Then the events of the previous night came flooding back. He breathed more easily when he saw the door of the cell lying wide open. He grimaced as he felt his swollen and bruised throat.

Hearing some movements in the front office, he went through to find Luke frying bacon and eggs on the old stove that stood in the middle of the sparsely furnished room. The smell of freshly brewed Arbuckles wafted across to him from the grey steel coffee pot.

'Sleep well?' asked Luke, looking up from his frying pan.

'Better'n most places I've stayed in,' said Jake, smiling at the old man.

'Safer too, probably. I usually breakfast at the saloon but I thought it better if we stayed out of sight this morning. Don't think we'd be the most welcome customers at one of Carter's places. Pump's out the back if you want to get cleaned up. Don't be too long though, breakfast's nearly up.'

By the time Jake came back into the office he found Luke just putting two large tin plates of food on his broad desk. They sat down and shared the hearty meal together, saying little, each lost in his own thoughts.

Within a short space of time the two men had found a healthy, mutual respect for each other. They knew, along with the unlikely hero in the guise of Neville Chuster, that they all needed each other if they were going to survive for any time against Jordan Carter.

They had sat up until the small hours of the morning going over their predicament but no clear plan of action had been agreed on. Before he had drifted off to sleep, Jake had pondered the odds. An old man and a pen-pusher against a team of professional gunslingers. He couldn't help but think this was only going to end one way, and yet he couldn't find it in his heart to abandon the two men who had risked their necks to save his.

He was just finishing his second cup of coffee when the office door swung open and Elaine McDonnell came rushing in. She stopped suddenly and straightened her hair when she saw Jake. Both men quickly rose to their feet.

'Morning, Sheriff.'

'Morning, Elaine. How are you?'

She gently fingered a black bruise on the side of her cheek but smiled broadly.

'A lot better than if Mr Chalmers here hadn't come along.'

She looked straight into Jake's eyes and for the first time in a long time he felt he had done something that actually mattered.

'Are you OK?' she said. 'I heard those dogs tried to hang you. Is that right?'

This time it was Jake who tenderly rubbed his wounds.

''Fraid so. I tried to get you out of a pickle and ended up having to be rescued by Luke and Neville. All in all, it was quite a night.'

She glanced down at the remnants of the meal and the open cell.

'I heard you'd been arrested. You don't look much like under arrest to me,' she said with a large smile of relief. 'Will you be leaving town now, Mr Chalmers?'

'Please, miss, call me Jake. No, I won't be leaving just yet. I've got some business that needs attending to.'

He looked sideways at Luke and Elaine caught the significance of their glance.

'Well, I'd best be going. I just wanted to say 'thank you' for what you did. And Pappy says you've to come for supper tonight. You and the sheriff and Mr Chuster.'

'Well, that's mighty kind of Abe. Tell him we'll be there,' said the sheriff with obvious pleasure. It had been a long time since he'd been invited to a proper family home.

'Thanks,' said Jake, 'that'll be fine.'

Elaine turned to open the door then turned round.

'I'm glad . . . you're not leaving, I mean . . . '

Embarrassed and a little surprised by her own frankness, she quickly left the office, banging the door behind her. The two men watched her go. The sheriff rubbed his chin thoughtfully.

'She'd make a pretty fine wife, young Elaine. All the young studs around here are chasing her but I ain't seen her show no interest in any of them — until now, that is!'

He laughed heartily as Jake turned a

bright shade of red.

The door had barely closed when it was flung open again. A young boy called Jimmy Nesbitt, Neville's printer's devil, was standing in the office gasping for air. His words came out in a breathless rush, tumbling over one another.

'Sheriff . . . Mr Chuster . . . sent me . . . you've to come . . . straight away . . . something terrible's happened!'

Luke and Jake grabbed their hats and quickly followed the boy across the street and down to the newspaper office. Outside, a crowd of spectators had already gathered, a buzz of murmuring hung over them as they craned their necks to get a better view of what had happened.

The once proud home of the *Sweetwater Chronicle* was now a sorry sight. The front windows were smashed, the door wrenched off its hinges. There were sheets of blank newsprint blowing in the street and along the boardwalk. Jake and the sheriff made their way into the office where they found Neville standing staring mournfully at his presses — or what was left of them.

Blocks of type were scattered all over the wooden floor like a child's discarded toys. Pipes and wheels belonging to the steam engine that had driven the press were twisted and broken. Black ink lay in pools under the press bed as though the machine, mortally wounded, was slowly bleeding to death. Stacks of newsprint lay ripped and scattered all over the floor and Neville's desk and chair had been smashed with axes. It was obvious that the *Sweetwater Chronicle* would not be doing much reporting for a while. Standing lost amongst the devastation, Neville stood gazing around him in disbelief.

Luke came up behind him and put his hand gently on his shoulder. Neville turned and gave a weak smile when he saw the two men.

'I'm sorry, Neville,' said Luke.

'My, they did a thorough job, didn't they?' murmured Neville.

'Can you put it together again?' asked Jake.

Neville sighed.

'I might. But what's the point? So they can come back and do it all again? It's taken me years to build this newspaper from nothing and it's back where I started in just one night.'

He stooped and lifted some torn handbills advertising a stock sale.

'Anyway, I'm not going to write another word unless it's the truth. Unless it's what I believe in. What sort of newspaper will the *Chronicle* be if I can write anything as long as it's OK with Mr Jordan Carter?'

'Put it back together, Neville,' said Luke quietly. 'You were right when you started the paper. We won't fix this town with guns. We need to tell the decent folk around here just what's been going on and what Carter plans to do to the place these people call their home.'

Neville gave a bitter laugh.

'Hearts and minds, eh, Sheriff? You

reckon the pen is mightier than the sword — or Jordan Carter's guns?'

'Yes, Neville. In fact, I do,' said Luke. He smiled at him reassuringly.

Neville stood staring at the press for a few more minutes. He stooped and lifted a few bits of broken pipe in one hand then picked up some pieces of type in the other. Sighing deeply, as though summoning some deep inner strength, he suddenly shouted out into the street.

'Jimmy . . . ' Jimmy . . . ?'

The boy ran in, out of breath and flushed.

'Yes, Mr Chuster?'

'Get a brush and big box for trash. We've got a lot of work to do. The *Chronicle* will hit the streets tomorrow as usual!'

9

It took most of the night for the three men and the boy just to clear the office of the worst of the broken debris. They separated what could be salvaged or repaired and what could never be used again. The sun had set and the night was black outside before the floorboards could be seen again and the small office had begun to resemble the busy newspaper press it had been before. They stood back and surveyed their work with a real sense of achievement and agreed that they had probably done enough for one night.

As they were trying to scrub off the dust and newspaper ink as best as they could in the buckets of cold water that Jimmy had brought in from the pump, Elaine timidly knocked at the door.

'If anybody's interested, there's plenty of home-cooked chow round at the livery stable. It's on the table now and getting cold.'

No one needed a second bidding. Eagerly the men followed her out of the newspaper office and down the street to the small cabin that joined the livery stable and was what Abe and Elaine called home.

The small kitchen was warm from the heat of the large black range that lined almost one wall. The air was filled with delicious smells of fried pork, mashed potatoes, freshly baked corn bread and brewed coffee. Kerosene lamps dotted around the room made it feel cosy and safe. The men quickly took their places on the benches around the large pine table and started eagerly disposing of the spread while Elaine fussed over them like a mother hen and made sure there were plenty of second helpings. For a time, it seemed their troubles were forgotten and soon the cabin was filled with the sound of talk and laughter.

As he ate, Jake looked around the

table. For the first time in a long time, he was with people whom he liked and trusted and who seemed to need him in return. It was hard to believe that just a few days ago he had blown into this town as a total stranger. Now here he was, surrounded by people he would be proud to call his friends, but still there was that nagging voice in the back of his head that kept telling him he was breaking every rule he'd ever made for himself. He was getting involved. He was getting dragged into these people's affairs when it didn't have to be his concern. Every instinct told him he should go. He could slip out, saddle up and disappear like a ghost in the night. What was it that was holding him back?

He felt his arm being roughly nudged.

'What's the matter, boy?' said Abe. 'You're a million miles away. Come on. Eat up!'

Abe McDonnell now treated him as a hero for saving his daughter and Elaine seldom took her eyes from him, which he found welcome and uncomfortable at the same time.

Around the table the conversation, of course, eventually returned to Carter, his men and the plans he had for Sweetwater. They all agreed that everyone in this room was now on the wrong side of Carter's ambitions and would soon have him to reckon with. The debate ranged far and wide but there was no real decision reached on how to best deal with the situation. Soon the conversation dwindled as the men lit their pipes and sat with their second or third cups of coffee around the fire, thoughtfully staring into the depths of the orange flames.

As Elaine cleared the things from the table, Jake stood up and stretched.

'I think I'll just check up on Paulo,' he said.

He crossed in darkness to the stables and let himself in. Paulo was standing gently nibbling some fresh straw and looked fresh and groomed, his coat shimmering in the soft light of a nearby kerosene lamp. He snickered and shook his mane as Jake gently rubbed his nose and patted his mane.

'How are you, boy? You OK?'

As though in answer to the question, Paulo nodded his head and pushed his muzzle against Jake's chest almost knocking off him balance.

'You look as though you're pretty settled here, ain't you? Well, don't start getting too cosy cos I don't know how long we'll be hanging around. I don't know if the likes of you and me belong here. What do you think?'

'I think he's a lot happier than you are,' said a voice from the door.

Jake swung round and saw Elaine standing in the doorway. He didn't know how long she'd been standing there but she'd obviously heard what he had been saying to Paulo. She made her way across the stable floor to stand beside him. She put her hand on Paulo's flanks, and then turned to look Jake straight in the eyes.

'You're a strange one, Jake Chalmers.

Just what is that makes you such a restless soul? I've been watching you all night. You can't settle. Even when you're sitting still, your mind is somewhere else. What is it that you are so afraid of? What is it that makes you so scared of getting . . . close?'

'I guess I'm just made that way,' said Jake, uncomfortable with her questioning.

'I don't think so,' she persisted. 'I think something happened to make you this way. What happened to you, Jake?'

And then, for the first time since it happened, he felt himself telling this girl with the deep-blue eyes what had happened on that day when he was just fourteen years of age that was to change his life for ever.

He told her how, nearly ten years ago, he was heading into town with his ma and pa. They were going to pick up their regular provisions, the same as they had done every month for as long as he could remember. Sitting up front in Pa's old buckboard, they were laughing and singing the psalms his ma loved to sing in church on a Sunday.

'It's about the last time I can remember being truly happy,' said Jake.

He broke off and stared into the distance of his memory. Elaine reached out to touch his arm.

'What happened, Jake?'

'We were in town for a couple of hours. While Pa hauled sacks of salt, flour and sugar into the back of the buckboard, Ma liked to look in the shop windows at all the fancy new dresses and the latest new-fangled kitchen gadgets just in from the East. I used to wander along to the general store and stare at the rows of jars of candy.' He smiled. 'I'd never seen so much candy in all my life.'

'Go on, Jake,' said Elaine.

'Well, all of a sudden I heard my pa's voice in the street. I ran out of the store and I saw him facing up to a couple of drunken cowboys who'd picked a fight over something stupid like a space at the hitching rail. I'd never seen my pa angry before. He tried to reason with them — he wasn't afraid; he just didn't want to fight. He even offered to move the buckboard but the cowboys kept goading him on. They told him to draw his gun but he didn't carry one. I'd never seen him use one other than for hunting.'

He turned to face Elaine. Her faced was etched with concern.

'You see, Elaine, he believed we didn't need them. He believed in the law and justice. He made me promise I'd never carry one either.'

His hand reached down and touched the carved leather of his holster.

'Guess I didn't keep that promise, did I?'

'Go on,' said Elaine knowing there was a lot more to come.

'I was nearly level with them when I heard the shot. Then everything happened so quick. My pa fell into the dust. There was lots of screaming and people running for cover. Then next thing, my ma was kneeling in the dust beside my pa, screaming at him not to die. She was still holding him tight when they shot her too.'

Elaine put her hand to her mouth, the tears welling in her eyes.

'Well, the two cowboys rode out. Just like that. They were never caught. Never brought to justice for what they did.'

'What happened to you?' asked Elaine.

'Oh, neighbours took me in but I was too much of a handful for them. I was kinda angry all the time. I couldn't settle at anything. I got myself thrown out of school and started skipping chores on the farm. I made some money working where and when I could, and as soon as I'd saved up enough I got myself an old gun and a bucketload of shells. For hours on end, for months, I shot cans and bottles from fences until I guess I was pretty fast. Then I left the county and I've never been back.'

'Are you still angry, Jake?'

He stared at her for a while and then said, 'I guess I am. What I learned that day was that my pa was wrong and I suppose I was angry that he didn't carry a gun. That he didn't protect us. I learned that the only law people respect is the law of the gun.'

He looked down at the straw on the stable floor.

'I swear, I don't go looking for trouble, Elaine, but I always promised myself I'd be ready if it came and found me.'

Before he knew what was happening, she was in his arms. She put her arms around his waist and pulled tight. As she laid her head against his chest, he could smell the faint smell of lavender from her hair that gently brushed his face. He pulled his arms tighter around her and they stood for what seemed an eternity sharing each others heartache.

'Elaine? Elaine?'

Her father's voice calling in the night broke them apart. She smiled at him and they both made their way across to the cabin. When they got in, the men were standing around getting ready to leave. Neville was putting on his gold spectacles and slipping his arms into his jacket.

'Well, I sure would like to spend the rest of the night with you all just sitting here jawing, but I've got a newspaper to get rolling, so if you'll all just excuse me . . . '

'You're not going back to work at this late hour, are you?' said Abe.

'Looks like it.'

'Well, there's plenty of willing hands here. We'll come with you.'

'No, no,' said Neville, 'it's way too late.'

But they wouldn't hear of it and despite Neville's protestations, they made their way to the newspaper office, going in ones and twos, careful that any of Carter's men didn't see them.

Young Jimmy concentrated on putting the type racks back together in order while Neville worked on getting the steam engine fired up. Luke and

Abe set about mending the door and windows and getting some old furniture replaced. Jake generally helped out where he could and Elaine kept the coffee and biscuits coming. It was two o'clock in the morning before the place looked as though it just might be able to produce a newspaper again.

Eventually, Neville stood up from where he had been hunched over the steam engine and groaned as he straightened his back.

'OK, folks, let's call it a day. I want to thank you all for your help. I couldn't have done it without you.'

'What happens now, Neville?' asked Luke.

'Now?' Neville smiled. 'Now I sit down and hit back at Mr Jordan Carter.'

He patted the old black press lovingly.

'This, ladies and gentlemen, is my gun and the words I write are my bullets. I can hurt them as much as they've tried to hurt me. Tomorrow, the

Chronicle will rise like the phoenix from the ashes and people will hear its roar!'

Even though everyone was dead beat with tiredness, they broke into applause. Jake joined in impressed at this small, unimposing man's brave words — and secretly hoped he would not live to regret them.

10

It was barely sunup when Neville Chuster barged into Luke Gardner's office. He strode across and almost threw down the latest edition of the *Sweetwater Chronicle* on to the startled sheriff's desk.

'Read all about it! Read all about it!' he shouted, a broad grin stretched across his tired face.

'When did you do all this?' asked Luke, putting down his first cup of coffee of the day and lifting up the freshly printed pages.

'Been up all night. I was just itching to see if the press worked. A couple of columns are a bit off line and I've lost a few characters somewhere but all in all I'd say we've done a pretty good job.'

Jake came out from the cells tucking his shirt into his pants.

'Hey, what's all the fuss?'

'Come and see,' said Luke.

Both Jake and the sheriff scanned down the tightly packed columns of print. The leading story was a detailed description of how Jordan Carter and his men had tried to destroy the newspaper office. In big bold type across the top of the newspaper, the headline read:

JORDAN CARTER TRIES TO SILENCE THE VOICE OF THE PEOPLE

It went on to explain clearly what Jordan Carter had done to the town since he'd arrived and what the newspaper thought were his plans for the future. It was now time, the newspaper declared, for all decent-minded folk to rally round the town's sheriff and do everything in their power to resist him. On no account could Jordan Carter take over as the mayor of Sweetwater, and Neville urged someone to stand in opposition to him.

'What do you think?' asked Neville.

'Pretty strong stuff,' said Luke thoughtfully. 'This'll cost Carter a few votes by the time the election time comes around.'

'What do you think, Jake?'

'It's good,' said Jake but there was a strange look of doubt on his face. He put the paper down and walked over to the stove to get some coffee.

Luke rose to his feet.

'I'm going for a walk. Coming?' he said to Jake.

'No. I think I'll just hang around here a while, if you don't mind.'

'So you liked what I wrote in the paper, did you?' Neville said when Luke had gone.

'Yeah. Great.'

'What bit did you like the best?'

Jake came over to the table and scanned the paper.

'It's all good. It's great.'

'What? Even the bit about urging all the townsfolk to run out of town every cheap gun-toting killer who comes into Sweetwater, including you?'

'What?' said Jake, staring at Neville hard. 'You wrote that about me?'

Neville lowered his head and stared at his feet.

'Sorry, Jake. That was a lousy trick.' He looked up at the young cowboy. 'You can't read. Can you?' he asked quietly.

Jake was about to deny it then stopped himself.

'No, I can't read. After Ma and Pa . . . ' He stopped himself. 'I wasn't much interested in schooling and when I found I could sketch a couple of brands on a slate, I reckoned I'd learned all I needed to.'

He looked down at the rows of neatly spaced writing.

'The only thing I ever did learn to do well was to outdraw another man and take his life and put the fear of God into anybody who saw me do it. Like last night. I always wanted to read; just never got around to doing it. Guess it's too late for that now.'

'It's never too late,' said Neville, 'I

know there's a lot of other stuff going on just now, but if you're interested, I could help you. You come round to my place a couple of evenings a week and I'll have you reading and writing like a scholar in no time. You're a bright fellah, Jake. It'll be easy.'

'You'd do that for me?'

'Sure.'

Jake paused for a while then looked straight into Neville's eyes.

'You're a brave man, Neville. Guys like me look brave but it takes more guts to do what you're doing than for someone like me to get my gun out first and pull the trigger.'

'Don't call me brave yet,' laughed Neville, 'wait until Jordan Carter reads this and comes looking for me!'

The laughter died in his throat as the door bashed open and a group of men walked purposefully into the office. They were lead by Jeremiah Isaacs, the current leader of the town council, who held a copy of the morning's *Chronicle* crumpled in his fist. A bullish man, with a large red face and a bushy handlebar moustache, he was given to tempers and loud rhetoric and liked the sound of his own voice. He spoke with the conviction of a politician and usually managed to talk down anybody who had different opinions, but everyone knew he was Carter's puppet. He was also the owner of the general store and since Carter had swelled the number of hard-spending customers coming to Sweetwater his business was thriving. If Carter got his way he would make even more, so he was not about to tolerate anyone upsetting his particularly profitable apple cart. He waved the newspaper under Neville's nose.

'Ah, just the man I was looking for,' declared Isaacs in his booming voice so that the men at the back of the group could hear him as clearly as those at the front. 'What do you call this, Chuster?'

'It's today's newspaper, Isaacs,' said Neville calmly, determined not to be intimidated by Isaacs's manner. Jake was ready to step in and help him if he needed him but Neville looked more than able to deal with this blustering bully.

'I know it is. But what's all this stuff about Jordan Carter?'

'It's the truth. That's probably why you don't recognize it.' This caused some mutterings and a few sniggers from the men behind. Isaacs's face went a darker shade of pink. He wasn't used to being spoken to this way or having his authority challenged.

'Listen to me, Chuster. Your job is to report what goes on in this town. Not make up stories like some dime-novel writer.'

'Look, Isaacs. You may think you're somebody in this town but you don't tell me what to print in my paper. Jordan Carter couldn't shut me up and you won't be able to either.'

'You're making some pretty big enemies, Neville. Mr Carter ain't gonna like this.'

'Mr Carter isn't meant to like it.'

'Yeah? Well, we're going to Mr Carter

right now and tell him we don't back you and you do not represent the majority of the citizens of Sweetwater. We don't support you, the sheriff, or this two-bit gunslinger that shot down two of his men in cold blood. We just want a quiet life here. Why are you stirring things up?'

'You think things are quiet now? With Carter in control? With the law of the gun running this town? Carter wrecked my newspaper. He's trying to crush anybody who stands in his way. Today it's me. Tomorrow it could be you.'

'You have no proof it was Carter. It could just have been some of the boys hell-raising and things got out of hand. If the sheriff had been doing his job protecting law-abiding citizens' property instead of shielding murderers from the law it wouldn't have happened.'

There was a chorus of agreement behind him.

'I can't believe you're all closing your eyes to what's happening,' said Neville in exasperation. 'I've written the truth about what happened last night and I'll continue to write the truth as long as there's breath in my body. Carter can't buy me . . . '

Isaacs's eyes narrowed at Neville's insinuation but he brushed it aside.

'Well, don't say we didn't warn you. You're on your own. Come on, boys.'

Neville watched Isaacs and his small band of followers leave the office and go across the road. Halfway across, Jeremiah crumpled up the newspaper and threw it into the street.

Neville felt sorry for them but he felt frightened as well. He had thought that if he took a stand he would get support from people like that. But now it looked as if his ploy had backfired on him, digging himself, Luke and Jake deeper into this already murky hole.

'There goes an angry man,' said Jake as he watched the men cross the street.

'Oh, yes, we haven't heard the last of Jeremiah Isaacs,' murmured Neville as he watched a sheet of his newspaper lying in the dirt and flapping gently in the wind.

11

It didn't take Jordan Carter long to get his own copy of the *Sweetwater Chronicle*.

He read it in silence but his dark brows knitted close together, his temper gathering slowly like an impending storm. Sitting in his red-leather armchair, one of many that decorated his opulent room above the Eldorado, his only movement was the occasional puff of blue smoke from the large cigar jammed between his clenched teeth.

The room was dark and cool. Long, green, heavy velvet curtains kept out the worst of the day's glare and dampened the noise that filtered in from the busy street down below but Jordan Carter was oblivious to everything except the small printed words in the newspaper he held in his hands.

When he had read the lengthy article

all the way through he slowly stood up. He folded the newspaper carefully into half and then half again and then gently laid it down in the centre of his broad mahogany desk. He took one last deep draw on his cigar and then stubbed it out repeatedly in a brass ashtray until the red glow had completely disappeared.

Lance Gurney stood at the window looking out into the street, watching everything and nothing in particular. Nate Jordan sat across from his brother on a low settee. They waited expectantly. Neither wanted to catch the older man's eyes. They knew him well enough to know that this was no time for idle conversation and the wrong word would only bring his wrath down on them. At last, after what seemed an age, Carter turned to Gurney.

'I thought you said you'd put this guy out of business,' he said quietly.

Lance shuffled his feet uncomfortably on the carpet.

'I thought we had. I thought we'd

fixed him good and proper. Honest, Mr Carter, we left that place looking like a tornado had swept thought it. We smashed his machine to pieces. Didn't we, Nate?'

Nate nodded but said nothing.

'Obviously not enough pieces,' snarled Carter.

He turned to stare at the newspaper on his desk.

'Not only has he managed to get his pathetic little rag together again, he's obviously not getting the message. If he thinks he can trash my reputation in this town and get away with it, he'd better think again! This newsman is proving to be a real irritation . . . '

He drummed perfectly manicured fingers on his desk for a few minutes before turning to the two men.

'I need you to pay our local newspaper office another little visit; and this time I want him out of business permanently. But I don't want to be connected. I don't want anything that points the finger back to me, d'you both understand?'

The two men nodded.

'This time make it look like an accident.'

'What sort of an accident?' asked Nate.

Carter didn't answer. He stared at the newspaper on his desk again, then lifted it by one corner between two fingers. With his other hand, he struck a match and lit the bottom corner. For a minute, nothing happened, and then a yellow flame flared and quickly made its way up one edge of the newspaper. When it started to lick near his fingers, he dropped it into a trashcan beside his desk, where it writhed and curled until the flames died into tortured black ashes. He looked up at the two men.

'Burns well, don't it?' He smiled.

Nate nodded and looked across at Lance. An evil grin spread across the two men's cruel faces.

They knew exactly what they had to do.

12

Neville didn't waste any time in getting a slate, some books and chalk so that Jake could get started on his lessons. Neville promised that no one else need know what they were doing and that night they sat in the office until midnight going over the alphabet again and again.

Jake felt stupid and slow but Neville was patient and a good teacher and keen to get Jake to learn. They sat round the single oil lamp, Neville reading, Jake practising letters on a slate. The room that doubled as Neville's office and bedroom was warm and snug, the heavy shades drawn down. Every now and again, Jake looked up from his slate and glanced at the rows of books surrounding the room stacked on roughly made shelves and wondered if he would ever be able to read them.

'It'll come,' said Neville, guessing his thoughts.

Jake smiled and bent over again to his task.

'Want more Arbuckles?' asked Neville, going over to the stove where a coffee pot gently steamed.

'No thanks,' said Jake, reaching back and stretching. 'Think I'll call it a night. This learning stuff's harder work than a day's branding.'

Neville laughed. 'You'll get used to it.'

Jake was gathering his bits and pieces together when suddenly he grabbed Neville's arm and motioned him to keep quiet. Neville looked perplexed. He hadn't heard anything.

Jake drew his Colt slowly from the holster and made towards the back door that lead into the alley. He pointed to the lamp, motioned to Neville to turn it down then follow him with it. As Neville was doing this, he heard what Jake had heard. A scraping sound coming from the small lane which ran just alongside the office. Then nothing; then the small bang of a tin drum.

Jake stood by the door listening carefully, then slowly he turned the round brass handle. Whoever was out there, they probably thought everyone was asleep and Jake and Neville could now clearly hear the slopping sound of liquid being carelessly splashed around.

Jake opened the door silently and slid into the gloom of the alleyway. He motioned Neville to follow him quietly. They stood in the darkness and let their eyes grow accustomed to the gloom. Soon they could clearly make out the large silhouette of Lance Gurney slopping kerosene over the dry wooden walls of the *Sweetwater Chronicle*.

The can was already almost empty. Lance shook out the last couple of drips then put the can down and fumbled in his vest pocket.

'Looking for a light?' asked Jake quietly from the darkness.

Lance wheeled round just as Jake

cocked the trigger of his Colt, discouraging any thoughts that Lance might have had of going for his gun. Neville turned the kerosene lamp up and Lance blinked in the light.

'I think you should drop your gunbelt real slow and then we'll go along to the sheriff's office and you can explain just what you were doing,' said Jake quietly.

At first Lance looked as though he was going to obey, then his hand went instinctively for his gun. Jake could have beaten him easily if Neville hadn't been there. Instead he tried to push Neville out of the way and pull his gun at the same time. Neville fell heavily against the wall and the oil lamp fell from his grasp plunging the lane into darkness. Lance's two shots lit the alleyway in brilliant flashes, both bullets disappearing into the wooden wall closely behind Jake. On the ground, a small blue flame from the broken lamp found the spilt kerosene and started to snake its way silently along the liquid.

Lance was standing in a puddle of

the fuel when the flame hit it. Both Jake and Neville shielded their eyes against the ball of yellow flame into which Lance disappeared. He screamed hideously, writhing in pain and terror as his clothes began to disintegrate in the inferno.

'Get a blanket, Neville, get a blanket!' screamed Jake. He ran forward and pushed Lance out into the street, burning his hands and singeing his face as he did so. He tripped Lance up and, as he fell awkwardly, Jake started to roll him on the ground, scooping handfuls of dust in two hands and spraying it over him like water. Neville ran up with a blanket and together they wrapped the whimpering man until the flames were doused.

Through all of this, they didn't see the slight figure of Nate Carter edge his way out of the shadows and start to run up the main street towards the Eldorado.

A small crowd, alerted by the shouts and screams, beginning to gather around the three men. They stopped and stared at what they had first thought was a bundle of rags, and then realized it was the charred and burned body of Lance Gurney. The fire was out, but his life had almost gone out with it.

He was barely conscious but he still flinched in agony as they tried to pull the blanket back to see the extent of his wounds. With a sickening jolt, Jake realized that, as he pulled the blanket back, Lance's skin was slowly peeling with it.

'Get Doc Fisher!' shouted Jake and someone ran off into the night to get him. Lance's eyes opened but they were focused somewhere far off, unaware of his surroundings. He raised his hand blindly into the air and when Neville took it, he gripped it so hard he winced with the pain.

'Don't let me die — please — don't let me die.'

'We're getting the doc, Lance. It's gonna be OK. Just try and lie still.'

Neville looked up at Jake who shook his head. He'd seen burns like this before once in a bunkhouse fire. Jake knew he wouldn't make it through the night. He leaned across Lance's ash-streaked face.

'Why did you do this, Lance? Who put you up to it?'

Lance stared with unseeing eyes up into the night sky. He started to speak but his words were lost in a fit of choking that racked his broken body. Eventually, when he managed to speak, he spat the words out with hatred.

'Carter. Carter told me to burn it down.'

'Why?'

'Those things you wrote about him. He was real mad.'

Lance convulsed in pain again, and he let out a whimper but whether it was pain or fear or both it was hard to tell. Jake didn't want to ask him any more questions — it wasn't right — but Lance had more to say.

'I wasn't here on my own . . . Nate

. . . he was here too . . . he ran off . . . left me to die . . . I can't believe . . . we were meant to be pals . . . '

The word faded on his lips. By the time Doc Fisher had hurried to the scene, Lance Gurney had done his last piece of dirty work for Carter. Neville and Jake, blackened with smoke, kneeled beside him. Eventually, Doc Fisher pulled a corner of the blanket over Lance's face, hiding his staring eyes. Slowly, the two men stood up. Then, Neville turned and started shouting.

'The office — it's on fire!'

Yellow flames were slowly licking up the side of the timber building. He ran back into the alley, slipped off his jacket, and started to beat the flames that were crawling up the walls. Jake rounded up a few of the bystanders and got them to grab pails and anything else that would hold water. He started getting them to lift water out of a nearby horse trough. Soon, they had a small but effective chain going and there was a steady stream of water being thrown over the building.

Eventually, the flames were put out. Although the building was blackened with smoke the walls were not damaged much. Jake and Neville stood back, wiped their smoke-blackened faces and smiled at each other.

For the second time in two days, the *Sweetwater Chronicle* had been saved but both men wondered when Jordan Carter would try again.

13

The next morning Luke Gardner stood outside the sheriff's office and looked up and down Main Street. For the first time in a very long time he felt like the upholder of the law in Sweetwater again. It had taken a young upstart, a stranger, to remind him of the pride in the job he used to live for. He had forgotten how good it was to walk through this town and have people respect you and look to you for reassurance and help.

It was good to feel too, that the silver badge on your lapel still stood for something and not just because of the badge. It had taken him a long time to learn what he had known from the beginning — that the badge was only as good as the person who wore it.

By the time he'd arrived at the newspaper office last night, Jake and

Neville had got things under control but today was when he played his part.

Lance Gurney's dying confession had been heard by a crowd of witnesses and it was now time to bring this town back under the control of the law. What better way than bringing one of the Carters to justice?

He hadn't let Jake or Neville in on his plans, especially Jake. He wanted to do this by himself so that no one could accuse him of hiding behind a gunslinger. Wouldn't that make him just as bad as Carter? Jake was a good man to have around in a tight fix but it was time for the law to be upheld and that was his job.

Luke walked up quiet Main Street. When he reached the Eldorado he paused outside, took a deep breath and then swung the batwing doors open. Half a dozen of Carter's crew turned round with mild interest when he walked in. Nate was leaning arrogantly on the bar.

'Well, 'morning, Sheriff. What can we

do for you? Breakfast is over and it's a bit early for liquor, even for you.'

He sniggered and some of the men around him laughed. Luke walked across and stood in front of the young man.

'Nate Carter, you're under arrest.'

There was a silence. A deep, dark silence as the men looked at him with a mixture of disbelief and hatred on their faces. It was broken by a high-pitched nervous giggle from Nate that grew into a loud derisive laugh. The tension shattered, the others joined in. Tentatively at first, then louder, until they were all guffawing loudly at the sheriff. Luke waited patiently until the laughter had run its course.

'Well, I'll tell you, Sheriff. I always had you marked out as a bit of a clown but now I find you're a comedian too. That's the best joke I've heard for a long time!'

'I'm mighty glad you guys find that funny, Nate, but you're coming with me.'

'Where to, Sheriff?' asked Nate mockingly, making no move from his perch in the bar.

'To the jail. I told you. You're under arrest.'

'For what?'

'The arson attack on the newspaper office for a start. You were there. Lance told us everything.'

'Lance? He's dead. Shot down in cold blood by your gunslinger partner. He's beginning to make a habit of cutting innocent men down in the street. If anyone should be thrown into jail it should be your trigger-happy buddy, not us.'

There were nods of agreement from the bar room. Luke ignored them.

'Before he died he identified you. In front of witnesses. It was the testimony of a dying man.'

Nate looked at the old man with cold eyes.

'I don't care what he said. I wasn't there and I didn't do anything. I ain't going nowhere with you.'

'Nate,' said the sheriff patiently, as though he was talking to a child, 'you come peaceably or, if I have to drag you down there, I will. It's up to you.'

Nate turned round and placed two elbows on the bar behind him. The men on either side of him took a couple of paces away. They had seen this happen before.

'Well, I guess I'd like to see you try and do that, Sheriff.'

Luke took a couple of steps towards him to show him he meant business, then stopped suddenly as he heard the rattle of the saloon doors swinging open. Thinking it might be one of Nate's cronies sneaking up behind him, he swung round, drawing his gun from his holster.

It was only young Jimmy Nesbitt, delivering more copies of the latest edition of the *Chronicle*. Luke smiled a brief smile of recognition and relief but it only stayed for a brief second before tightening into a hideous grin as blinding pain racked his body.

The gunshot was still reverberating and smoke was still lazily spiralling out of the muzzle of Nate Carter's gun as Luke Gardner, slowly, achingly, sunk first to his knees and then lowered himself gently on to the sawdust covered floorboards of the Eldorado. He looked up through glassy eyes and tried to focus on the ashen face of young Nesbitt as it disappeared from the top of the door. His shrieks could be heard as he ran down the street to get help.

He seemed to lie there for ever before he heard voices and footsteps return though the doors. When Neville and Jake made it to the saloon, Luke was already beyond the point of no return. Jake sank to his knees and cradled the old man, lifting his head on to his thigh.

'Luke? Luke? Can you hear me?' asked Jake urgently. Luke's eyes flickered open and with great effort focused on the young man's face above him.

'Take the badge, Jake,' whispered Luke, so quiet and far away that Jake had to put his ear to Luke's dry and cracked lips to catch the words.

'Luke. That's not important right now. We need to get you to a doctor. We need to get you patched up.'

Gardner coughed and grimaced. He slowly rocked his head from side to side. 'Waste of time, Jake . . . no time . . . '

'You'll be fine once we get you to a doc.'

'Jake . . . please . . . listen . . . the badge.' Luke's strength was fading but the urgency on the old man's voice was unmistakable. Jake gently undid the clasp of the badge and removed it from the lapel of the old man's leather vest. He held it in the palm of his hand gently, like a fallen bird, and showed it to Luke.

'Put . . . it . . . on . . . ' wheezed Luke.

Jake looked at him quizzically as though he didn't understand what the old man's intentions were.

'Put it on. I'll swear you in . . . '

Jake shook his head slowly.

'I can't do that, Luke. I can't be sheriff of this place. I don't belong here.'

From somewhere deep down the old man found the strength to reach up and grasp Jake's wrist tightly, so tightly that Jake felt the pain of it. He was glad of the pain though, as each moment passed, he felt the grip weaken.

'You . . . you're the one . . . to fix this . . . save Sweetwater, Jake . . . save 'em . . . '

Jake looked into the old man's eyes. He looked up and caught Neville and Elaine staring at him earnestly. Suddenly the small silver badge in his hand felt like an anvil. A few days ago nobody owed him anything and he owed other people even less. Now the whole future of a town and its people rested on his shoulders. His first instinct was to turn his back and ride out but he made himself look at the old man lying on the floor, his blood making a dark puddle around him and he knew he would stay.

The way Luke was going to die, gunned down mercilessly by a young coward, brought back that day fourteen years ago when he'd watched his ma and pa die the same way. Then, he had been too young to do anything about it. Now he could. Suddenly, he felt an angry fire burn deep in his soul and every fibre in his body cried out for this injustice to be avenged.

He knew he could not leave Sweetwater until he repaid the debt of friendship he had been shown, but he swore that when that debt was paid he would leave the future of the town in the hands of people who wanted the job. He could then ride out and vow never to be chained by friendship or — he looked up at Elaine — by love again.

He felt Luke shake his wrist and bring him back from his private thoughts.

'Jake . . . not much time . . . '

'OK, Luke old man,' whispered Jake kindly. 'You take it easy. I'll do it. I'll get the Carters out of Sweetwater and then you can have your badge back when I'm finished.'

A Bible was hurriedly found. As Jake held it in his right hand, Luke swore him in. It must have taken every sinew of strength, every ounce of last reserve to do it, for after Jake had agreed to uphold the law and his duty, the old man closed his eyes and his head rolled to the side. Whoever Jake would hand the town back to, it would not be Luke Gardner.

Jake let the old man's head fall gently on to the floor, then slowly he stood up. Without a word or a glance he pushed his way through the batwing doors of the saloon, through the murmuring crowd of folk who had gathered at the sidewalk and set off towards the sheriff's office.

14

Elaine covered Luke's body in an old stained tablecloth they found behind the bar. While she stayed with him Neville went off to find Hank Bellows, the undertaker. In less than an hour, they watched Luke's body being lifted into the back of Hank's black wagon and taken slowly down to his makeshift morgue, to be prepared for burial later that day. Although they did not voice their thoughts, Elaine and Neville knew they were both thinking about Jake. Both of them were silently afraid of what the tall quiet stranger would do next.

They both made their way to the sheriff's office, where they found him sitting behind Luke's old desk, his Colt in his hand and an open cartridge box beside his gunbelt and holster. He didn't look up when they entered but kept intently shoving slugs into his belt until it was filled. Neither of his friends had to ask him what he was doing but Neville uttered the words anyway.

'What are you going to do, Jake?'

Jake didn't reply. He looked up as though seeing his two friends for the first time. They both could see his eyes were filled with anger and a distant, faraway look that they had never seen before. Elaine walked over beside the desk and looked down at him.

'Jake? You're not thinking of going down there and tackling those boys head on, are you?'

Jake nodded. When he spoke, there was a slight tremor in his voice but only a fool would have mistaken it for fear.

'I'm the sheriff, ain't I? That's what you all wanted. A town sheriff's been gunned down and now it's my job to run the killer in. I'm going to see that boy hangs for murder if it's the last thing I do.'

He stood up to wrap the gunbelt around his waist and, with a couple of deft movements, had it buckled securely. He slipped the Colt into the holster and adjusted it so that it sat just right, low on his hip, ready for drawing. Elaine suddenly reached out and put her hand on his wrist. She stared into his eyes.

'Then what, Jake? After you've done that — you think that'll be the end of it?' she said, desperation edging her voice.

Jake looked at her calmly.

'After that,' he said quietly, 'I'll quit. It'll be the end of it. I'll have done my bit, paid my dues to Luke. I came from nowhere, I can disappear again. I've spent all my life blowing with the wind and I guess that's what I'll do for the rest of it. It's just the way I am, Elaine, and no good pretending otherwise.'

Suddenly, Elaine could no longer hold back the tears that were brimming in her eyes and she felt them burn as they coursed down her cheeks. She gripped his wrist tighter, willing him to listen to reason.

'You don't mean that, Jake. You know

you don't. It doesn't have to be this way. You don't have to do this. Neville, please, make him see . . . '

Jake looked down at her and his eyes softened. He would have done anything not to see her cry, to take her in his arms and just hold her close the way he had in the livery stable. For a moment he thought about taking his words back, but instead he reached out and gently but firmly lifted her hand away from his.

'I'm sorry, Elaine. I didn't mean it to be like this. I tried to tell you — '

'Jake! No . . . please don't go . . . '

As he made his way to the door, sobs broke from her throat. She sank into the chair and laid her head on her arms. Neville gave Jake a brief, grim smile as he passed him, opened the door and walked out of the office into the street.

The noon sun was high and hot but that was not the only reason Sweetwater's Main Street was almost empty. By now, everyone would have heard about Luke Gardner and knew there would be repercussions before this day was out. Keeping his eyes fixed directly ahead of him, Jake strode purposefully down the middle of the street and didn't stop until he'd walked through the swing doors of the Eldorado.

The place was quiet. No music — just small groups of men huddled round tables or leaning on the bar. They looked up as he walked in and he stopped. A quick glance round with eyes of cold steel confirmed that Jordan Carter was not among them. He walked through the tables and made his way to the stairs that led to the upstairs floor where he knew Carter had his office. One of Carter's men lounged at the bottom of the stairs but was obviously keeping guard to prevent anyone going up. He watched Jake approach but made no move.

As Jake drew level, the guard raised his hand. He was about to tell Jake that he couldn't pass but didn't get to utter a word before Jake's open hand flew at his face. Gripping his jaw tightly, with one lightning movement Jake thrust the man's head backwards. There was a sickening thud as the man's head bashed against the wooden banister, then he slumped to the floor, senseless.

Without breaking step Jake took the stairs two at a time until he reached the landing. At the top of the stairs he stopped, looking up and down the red-carpeted corridor. To his left the last door was marked PRIVATE. Jake walked straight towards it and, without hesitation, lifted his boot and kicked it. The door swung back violently, splinters of wood flying from the broken lock.

Jordan Carter was sitting behind his plush desk. Nate was sitting across from him, lying back in a soft chair. Both men wheeled round when they heard the door bang open but only Nate slid to the edge of his seat in fear. The elder brother sat motionless, fixing Jake with a hate-filled, steady gaze.

Jake scanned the room and, satisfied that there were no more of Carter's henchmen present, turned and looked at Nate's smug features. He felt fury rise in his chest. He took a deep breath and forced the anger to abate. He had learned that he had to stay in control and not do anything he would later regret through emotion; but still that fury tinged his voice.

'Get on your feet, boy,' he growled quietly.

Nate looked fearfully across to his elder brother, searching for guidance. Jordan raised his hand, indicating to him not to move.

'Stay where you are, Nate,' said Jordan calmly, like a man used to giving orders. He looked up, his eyes resting on the silver badge on Jake's vest lapel as he took a long slow pull on his cigar and let the smoke leak from the side of his mouth in long, hazy curls.

'Well, well,' he eventually said, 'the sheriff is dead — long live the sheriff. It sure didn't take you long to fill a dead man's boots.'

Jake ignored him. He continued to

stare at Nate who watched the two men alternately like a caged, frightened animal. Jordan kept on speaking.

'This sure is an interesting situation, Jake. You know, from the first time I met you, I had you marked as the kind of man I think I could do business with. I've been thinking that with my influence and your . . . 'abilities' . . . we could really sew this town up.'

He stubbed his cigar into a stone ashtray on his desk and sat back in his chair.

'It was a terrible thing that happened to Luke but in a way he had it coming. I tried to convince him but he never really saw the potential of the place. He had no imagination. Now you, Jake, I think you're made of different mettle. So what do you say, Jake? Think we can work something out?'

Jake slowly turned his head.

'I'm not here to do business, Carter. I'm going to make sure that this lily-livered skunk of a brother hangs for the murder of a federal sheriff. He shot a good man in the back who was only trying to do his duty.'

'Now wait a minute, Jake. Nate was being arrested for something he didn't do. It was self-defence. Luke had drawn his gun on him.'

'Tell it to the judge. I'm not here to discuss it. I'm taking him in and I don't think you or anybody wants to get in my way.'

Carter smiled and stood up.

'Really, Jake? You think you can take my kid brother out of here and I'm just going to stand by and let you? You're crazy. There's a saloon full of men downstairs who'll cut you to pieces before you get to the street. You don't stand a chance.'

He brushed a fleck of ash from the lapel of his velvet jacket and adjusted his white cuffs.

'Now, let's try and be reasonable. I'm sure, with a little give and take, there's bound to be some sort of agreement we can reach.'

'I'm not here to negotiate. You might

think you can wheel and deal your way out of anything, but not this time. I don't want anything you think you can give me. Everything you touch ends up dripping with blood. I ain't for sale.'

'You're mighty squeamish for a killer, Chalmers.'

Jake's eyes narrowed and his mouth tightened into an angry black line.

'I'm not proud about some things I've done, Carter, but I've never yet killed a man who wasn't going to kill me. Now I'm done talking.'

He turned to Nate.

'Get on your feet, son. I ain't gonna ask you again.'

Nate looked anxiously across at his elder brother who, this time, nodded slowly. Nate rose to his feet, the fingers on his right hand instinctively flexing.

'Drop the gunbelt slowly and don't even think about going for it,' warned Jake. 'I'm not going to turn my back on you so you can gun me down like you did Luke.'

'I could take you. You're not that fast,' said Nate as beads of nervous sweat began to shimmer on his top lip.

'Don't, Nate!' warned Jordan. 'We'll deal with this another way. Right now — do as he says.'

'But I could take him, Jordan . . . I could take him right now . . . ' Nate's voice was rising excitedly.

'You'd better listen to your brother,' said Jake, 'I'll take you in dead or alive. It doesn't matter to me. You're going to hang anyway — '

Before he'd finished the sentence, Nate had gone for his gun. It was barely out of his holster, when Jake's Colt leapt into his hands and a single shot rang out. As Jordan fell back against the wall, Nate fell to his knees with a terrified scream. His gun spun out of his hand and lay under a chair out of harm's way. He rocked back and forward holding his shattered right hand as blood rolled through his fingers, staining the expensive Paisley-patterned rug.

'Now get on your feet and move over towards the door,' said Jake, waving his gun.

'You crazy sonofabitch,' spat Jordan, all self-control gone.

'Get on your feet, boy, or I'll take out the other hand.'

He cocked the hammer to underline that he would do as he said, although the two brothers were now in no doubt that this man was capable and prepared to carry out his threats. Climbing unsteadily to his feet, the boy stumbled dazedly towards the door, clutching his hand against his chest where a large patch of blood was spreading. Jake kept his gun moving between the two men.

'All right, Carter. I'm giving you fair warning. If you or any of your heroes downstairs make a move on me I'm going to finish this boy. Understand?'

Nate was in tears. He turned to his elder brother.

'Jordan . . . help me. Don't let him take me . . . '

Jordan's face was pale with suppressed fury. He nodded reassuringly in the boy's direction but never took his eyes from Jake.

'Go ahead, boy. Do as he says. I'll sort this out. He won't get away with this.'

Nate passed through the door and Jake followed the sobbing boy to the top of the stairs. At the bottom, Carter's men had gathered. They had heard the gunshot but had not expected one of the Jordan brothers to be on the receiving end. As they made their way downstairs, Jake heard Carter's voice from the top of the landing behind him.

'Don't do anything, boys. Let him go.'

As they reached the bar room, men parted to let them pass, staring at Jake in amazement. As the two men went through the saloon's swing doors, Jordan Carter's voice followed them through.

'I'll get you, Chalmers! D'you hear me? You ain't gonna get away with this!

D'you hear me?'

Neither Jake or Nate stopped. They stepped off the boardwalk and, with his gun levelled, Jake prodded Nate in the back as they made their way down the main street towards the direction of the jail.

Elaine and Neville were waiting outside the sheriff's office. They too had heard the shot and had thought the worst. Elaine made to hug Jake as he passed but Jake shook his head.

'Go get the doc, will you?'

He walked Nate through to the cells at the back. He pushed him behind bars and told him to lie down on the bunk as he turned the heavy key, but Nate paced the confines of the cell, staring at him like a wild animal, a mixture of hate and fear in his eyes.

As Jake turned to go back into the office, Nate began to scream.

'You are a dead man walking! You think you're gonna get away with this? You have no idea what my brother is gonna do to you!'

Jake closed the connecting door and went into the office. As he put the ring of keys in the desk drawer, the boy's cries rang in his ears. Nate was right. Jake had no idea what Jordan Carter was going to do. He just hoped he would be ready when he did it.

15

The extraordinary general meeting of the Sweetwater town council had been hastily convened at Jeremiah Isaacs's general store at seven o'clock sharp that evening. It was very well attended. As usual, Jeremiah presided at the top table but, unusually for him, he was having little success in controlling the meeting, as emotions ran high.

Everyone in the room had either witnessed the events of the day for themselves or had heard the full story many times over from neighbours, friends and families. But no matter how they had come by their information, they were all now frightened and angry and shared the view that things had gotten way out of hand in Sweetwater. They had been happy to share in the newfound prosperity of the town but when their sheriff could be gunned down and then the murderer protected from justice, it was a price they were not prepared to pay. Now, they huddled together in their meeting room discussing the situation loudly but mostly demanding answers from the town council chairman.

'Hold on! Hold on!' shouted Jeremiah, trying to be heard above the mob. He banged his gavel on his makeshift meeting table. 'Folks! Folks! Can you all sit down? Can we bring this meeting to order? Can we?'

Eventually, everyone found somewhere to sit and the noisy conversations gradually abated until Jeremiah had their attention. He straightened his jacket and cleared his throat.

'Thank you, thank you. Now, I know what a lot of people are saying here tonight but we've got to get things into proportion. Now, what happened to Luke was terrible — just terrible — and of course, you're all right, we cannot tolerate the law being taken into the hands of one or two individuals.'

There were lots of nodding heads and shouts of agreement.

'But . . . but at the same time, we have got to do this properly. Now, I know that Jordan Carter's a reasonable man. I think that we can speak to him and make him see that he's overstepped the mark a little . . . '

'A little?' shouted someone from the back, and other people joined in.

'OK, OK. I agree. He's overstepped the mark, but I still say that we gotta handle things carefully.'

'I say we gotta fight fire with fire,' said another voice from the back. 'The only thing Jordan Carter understands is gunplay. I say we keep this Chalmers guy and get him to take Carter and his cronies on. What young Nate Carter needs is a short rope and a long drop!'

There were loud choruses of agreement but Jeremiah silenced them with a bang of his gavel.

'Now hold on. You can't have it both ways. I say that guy over there wearing Luke's badge is no better than one of

Carter's hired gunmen.'

'But he's the only law we've got!' someone said.

'He's *not* the law!' protested Jeremiah.

'Luke thought he was good enough to trust with his badge and that's good enough for me.'

There was a general murmur of agreement and much nodding of heads.

'Listen, listen to me, folks,' persisted Jeremiah. 'I understand emotions are running high. A lot's happened. Things are a bit uncertain, what with losing our sheriff and then those fellas holing out in the jail . . . '

Abe McDonnell was sitting in the front row of chairs and he now rose to his feet.

'We didn't 'lose' our sheriff, Jeremiah. It's not like he resigned or something. For God's sake, man, he was gunned down. Murdered like a dog. Shot down in cold blood. Are you gonna make peace with the man who did that?'

Jeremiah shook his head.

'I said I was sorry about Luke — I truly am. He was an old friend . . . but he shouldn't have tackled Jordan head on like that. He shouldn't have tried to arrest Nate!'

'Why's that, Jeremiah?' said Abe. 'You saying that the Carters are above the law?'

'No, but . . . '

The meeting again broke up into a mêlée of opinions and views, everyone talking at once to get their voices heard, but most were in support of Abe. Jeremiah banged his gavel again and again but this time, it seemed he had lost control despite his angry appeals for calm.

Then Ike Taylor, the local blacksmith, a large but gently spoken man, made his way to the front, pushing his way through the large group of people now standing and loudly debating the situation. He approached Jeremiah.

'Can I say something?' he asked quietly.

'Sure, Ike, sure,' said Jeremiah, glad to be no longer the focus of the crowd's attention.

A hush went through the room and everyone took their seats again as Ike turned to face them. He seemed uncertain, unused to talking in public, but determined to be heard. Hesitantly he began:

'Folks, I'd like to say a few words. I'm like most of you here. I got a business to run and a family to feed and I've not done too badly since the Carters started calling the shots. I've more business than I know how to handle sometimes with all them horses to be shod and wagons to be mended an' all. So rightly, I really haven't got anything to gripe about. I got a wife and four kids to feed and right now that ain't too much of a problem . . . but life ain't all about filling their bellies. I reckon there's more to just raising a family than that. They also got to grow up and help make Sweetwater a law-abiding town where they'll be safe and people can go about their lawful business without fear. Now Carter's been OK with us so far, but then again, it's suited him. But you don't know what the future holds. Look at Neville. Soon as Neville Chuster prints something about him that he don't like, Neville gets his livelihood wrecked. Luke Gardner was just doing his job and he was killed. Is that going to happen to me one day? Or you?'

He looked around the room. All eyes were on him. The young blacksmith's words were ringing home as true as his hammer on his anvil.

'Nate Carter murdered the lawman who swore to protect the citizens of Sweetwater. If he doesn't pay for that, then I don't know how we go on from here. We'll have turned our back on the sheriff and the town. We'll be saying that Sweetwater ain't worth fighting for and I believe it is. Now I don't know about other folks here, but I thought we were trying to build a town here. A community. A future for our children and their children. It seems to me that tonight we have a choice. We either live by the gun or the law. I know what I want it to be.'

The room was silent. Ike suddenly looked embarrassed as though he had woken from a dream and found it reality.

'I guess that's all I've got to say.'

He stepped away from the front of the room and sat down on the front row. A couple of hands patted him on the back. Every face now looked at Jeremiah expectantly. He looked around the room and then, as though realizing what he had to do, slowly nodded. He put down his gavel.

'I'll talk to him.'

As he pushed his way to the back of the store and disappeared through the doors into the street, people started to applaud.

16

Jordan Carter paced up and down the floor of his office like a caged animal. He was incensed at Jake's defiance. No-one treated him like this. No one! — and just as soon as he got his kid brother back he was going to make sure that Jake suffered for what he'd done.

If it hadn't been for that old fool of a sheriff, Jake would have already been strung up and out of the way. This time he'd make damn sure that no one would forget what happened to anyone who dared take on Jordan Carter.

Now all he had to do was work out how to get him out of that jail house without getting Nate killed too. That damned fool boy and his temper! He'd warned him about it a hundred times, but he was too headstrong by half. But he'd get him out of there and then keep him on a tighter rein in future.

Once this was over, once Jake and his little show of bravery was long forgotten, he was going to turn this town upside down. He'd put up with things for far too long now. Before he arrived this had been just a bunch of run-down buildings in the middle of nowhere. He'd built it up from nothing. Made a lot of people a lot better off in the process — and this was how they paid him back? Printing lies in the local rag, holding town council meetings about him? He'd let this stuff go on for too long and it was high time it was stamped out for good. He'd always dreamed of one day running for mayor. In his mind he'd even planned the election day with speeches, brass bands, with bunting hanging all the way down Main Street.

Well, he'd decided he wasn't going to do that. They'd had their chance. He was now going to do what he'd always done — he would just take it. Oh, he was sure there'd be a few protests about it but not to his face — they wouldn't dare — and then it would calm down when they realized this town couldn't survive without him. Once he'd dealt with Jake Chalmers, he would start about really sorting this town and then . . .

There was a timid knock at the door.

'Come in!' he shouted, angry at having his train of thought disturbed.

Jeremiah Isaacs walked into the room, fingering his hat nervously in front of him.

'Hi, Mr Carter. I, em, hope I'm not disturbing you or anything . . . '

Carter's first instinct was to throw the fat blustering idiot out of the room, but he decided to listen to what he had to say. He often had valuable information about what other people were getting up to that he used to ingratiate himself.

'What's wrong, Isaacs?'

'Nothing, really, Mr Carter. It's just that the town council had an emergency meeting tonight and there were a couple of things I thought maybe you should know about. Feelings are sure running mighty high . . . '

Jordan stared at him venomously. He'd make sure that this was their last meeting. No collection of traders and shopkeepers would tell him what he could and couldn't do with his town, but that would keep for later.

'What is it precisely you think I should know about?' he asked quietly.

'Well, I have to tell you, there was a lot of concern about the way Luke Gardner was . . . well, you know . . . '

Carter walked over to the window and stared out on to the deserted street below.

'Spit it out, Isaacs. I've got a few things to attend to.'

Jeremiah took a deep breath.

'Well, there ain't no easy way to say this, Mr Carter, but the folks feel that . . . well, what happened today is just not acceptable. You know, we understand you're sore about Nate and the way this fellah Chalmers arrested him but right now he's the only real law we got — official that is — and the town council demands that you leave him be until the judge settles this matter under the due process of law in the territory. Nate'll get a fair trial and . . . '

Carter walked across the room slowly as Jeremiah spoke, only pausing to lift a long silver letter-opener that sat on his desk. By the time he was face to face with him, the storekeeper had run out of breath.

'You finished?'

Jeremiah nodded nervously.

'You mind if I say a few things now?'

'Sure . . . sure . . . '

The next thing Jeremiah knew he was being roughly thrown against the door and pinned up against it while his windpipe was being cut off by Carter's steely grip and the letter-opener was being pressed hard up against his plump cheek. He felt the cold slice of metal and then the warm, slow trickle of blood.

'You *demand*, do you? You *demand*?' Carter's eyes were wild and filled with fury. 'You listen to me, you useless heap of lard, and you listen good. Without me you wouldn't even have a town! So you go back and tell them that I'm in charge and what I say goes and tell them never to 'demand' me to do anything ever again. *Never*! You got that?'

He shoved the knife deeper and Jeremiah let out a whimper of pain.

'I *am* the law around here and I say that damn sonofabitch holding my brother is gonna hang and whoever lifts a finger to help is gonna hang alongside him. I don't give a shit if I have to line both sides of Main Street down there with bodies until there's no one left. Now you'd better run along and take this message back to your chicken-shit town council and tell 'em this is their last meeting! And if you ever dare 'demand' anything of me again, you'll be Luke Gardner's new neighbour up in Boot Hill. Do I make myself clear?'

He let Jeremiah go and the grocer

sank to his knees, holding his throttled neck, gasping for air. Carter took a couple of steps back, then shouted for two of his henchmen. They came into the room and saw Jeremiah almost passed out on the floor.

'Gentlemen, I think Mr Isaacs could do with your assistance. He needs a little air.'

Jeremiah was lifted roughly, a hand under each arm and he half-stood, suspended between the two men, too weak to stand on his own two feet.

'I hope that's sorted everything out now, Mr Isaacs? Thanks for passing by. Get him out of here,' said Carter and then walked back over to the window overlooking the street.

As they made for the door he turned.

'Oh, and boys, make sure no further harm comes to Mr Isaacs on his way home, will you? There's some nasty varmints out there on the streets. You've got to be careful who you speak to.'

The men smiled and roughly bundled Jeremiah out on to the landing and to the top of the steep stairs. As he heard the loud thumps and cries as Jeremiah was thrown down the stairs, Jordan Carter's laugh became high and wild.

17

In the jail Doc Fisher carefully dressed the boy's wounded hand, then strapped it to his chest with a bandage that went over his shoulder and across his back. Nate wept with the pain and it was only after a large draught of laudanum took effect that he eventually slipped into a shallow and restless sleep. As the doctor washed his hands in a shallow pan of hot water, Elaine stood outside the cell door and watched over the boy closely, willing him not to die. She knew that, however bad things were now, if Jordan Carter's kid brother was to die here tonight, there would be no chance of anyone coming out of this thing alive.

'How is he really, Doc?' she said, coming up beside the old man as he dried his hands on a white linen towel.

'Well, his hand's shattered. Doubt he'll hold anything bigger'n than a pen again. And he's in shock. He don't handle pain too well, neither.' He smiled grimly when he saw the concern etched across the pretty young girl's face. 'But he's young and healthy and as long he doesn't go into a fever, he'll pull through. I'll leave some more laudanum and if the pain gets too bad, just top him up.'

Elaine put her hand on the old man's sleeve. 'Thanks, Doc,' she said, smiling.

'Anyway,' he said, 'Nate Carter is not my prime concern, young lady. I'm more worried about you. You know things are going to get a lot hotter around here, don't you?'

Elaine nodded as Doc Fisher reached out and took her hand. He lowered his voice and said, 'You need to get out of here, Elaine. This isn't your fight. I brought you into this world and I buried your ma and I know I'll be putting your pa right beside her if anything happened to you . . . '

'I'm fine, Doc, honest,' she said. 'You tell Pa that when you see him. I'll be all right as long as Jake's here.' She gave him a gentle peck on the side of the cheek and then went back to her vigil at the side of the cell.

As Doc Fisher shrugged his black frock-coat on to his shoulders he walked across to the two men who were guarding the front of the jail. Neville was nervously clutching a double-barrelled shotgun to his chest as he peered down the deserted street. Dusk was gathering.

Jake was at the other window, where he had stood watching the doc repair the boy's wound. Occasionally he glanced at Elaine, and when their eyes met he would give her a tight, tense smile to try and reassure her.

'How much do I owe you?' said Jake as the elderly doctor approached, snapping shut his small black medicine case.

'I'll bill it to the sheriff's office in the morning. That's what I used to do with Luke.' He hesitated slightly as he mentioned his friend's name.

'Thanks, Doc,' said Jakeand turned to the window again.

'Advice comes free, though, if you're interested?'

Jake turned round, his face emotionless. He nodded.

'I'm listening.'

'You're not going to last another twenty-four hours — you know that, don't you? Jordan Carter is not the type of man to let you get away with this. It's bad enough you've crippled his kid brother and I've no doubt he deserved a lot more after what he did to Luke. Luke was an old friend of mine and I'm as keen as the next man to see this kid get a hemp collar, but listen, son. To humiliate Carter in front of every citizen of this town is something he is gonna make sure you pay dearly for. I'm going to be back here tomorrow first light, but I'm feared it ain't gonna be the boy I'll be tending.'

He looked nervously over his shoulder to make sure Elaine hadn't heard him. She was still staring at Nate.

Jake nodded.

'Is there anything you want to tell me that I don't already know?'

'I just want to make sure you understand what you've got yourself into, son.'

A wry smile crossed Jake's face before he turned to check up Main Street again. 'It's crossed my mind once or twice.'

He turned to face the doc again.

'You said advice was free. So what's your advice?'

'Get out tonight. While you still can. While it's dark, get out and keep riding. Take Elaine with you. Her pa will understand. Make a new life for yourselves far from where Jordan Carter can reach you. I know you can handle yourself, boy, and I know you've probably never run away from a fight in your life, but trust me, this is one battle you're gonna lose.'

Jake turned to the window again.

'Thanks for the advice, Doc. Don't worry, I'll make sure Elaine gets outa here soon. But as for myself, you're right. I ain't never run away from a fight and I ain't about to start now; so you won't be hurt if I don't take your medicine, will you?'

The doc smiled as he made his way to the door.

'I thought you might have said that. I just wouldn't have felt right leaving without telling you. Good luck.'

He went out and snapped the door behind him. As his footsteps on the wooden sidewalk faded, an uneasy silence settled into the room. The only sound was Nate's loud breathing. Both men stared out of the window and Elaine seemed mesmerized by the small blue flame of the kerosene lamp that glowed on Luke's desk, getting stronger as the night drew in. For a while the three people in the room were separated by their own thoughts, fears and hopes.

When the grey dusk had faded to black, Jake's words shattered the silence.

'Well, you heard the doc. I guess it's time you were both going.'

Elaine spun round in her chair.

'Are you leaving tonight?' she almost cried.

'I told you, I'm not leaving until the circuit judge gets here. Then I can hand this dog over and I can be on my way.'

'But we can't leave you here. Not on your own!' protested Elaine.

'Looks like it. One thing's for sure, you two can't stay here. After I'm gone and I'm just a bad memory, you and Neville have got to live here among these people. You've taken my side too much already. You need to look after yourselves.'

Elaine was suddenly on her feet. Flushed and defiant, like an unbroken filly, the anger burned deep in her eyes. She stood with her hands on her hips.

'Now, you listen to me, Mr Jake Chalmers,' she said, 'you may be able to spend your entire life running away from responsibilities. Just picking them up when it suits you and throwing them away when they've served their purpose, but sometimes you've got to make a commitment to someone. Neville and me have made a commitment to you and we're sticking to it. You took that badge from Luke Gardner and now you think you can just walk out of here without a look backwards? Well, I'm not like that. I'm goin to stick through this until the end. Whether you like it or not!'

She pursed her lips together, barely under control, as though she was going to start crying again. Jake watched her impatiently. He was about to say something when Neville spoke.

'Looks like it's too late, anyway; there's a committee coming down the street headin' this way.'

Elaine went over beside Jake, who peered out into the gloom of the night. Lit by the soft glow of the gas lamps was a group of about a dozen shadowy figures all making their determined way up the main street towards the jail. They were led by the unmistakable figure of Jordan Carter. Jake cocked the Winchester.

'You know how to work one of these?' he asked Elaine.

'Sure. Sure I do.'

'A lot better than I do, I bet,' murmured Neville miserably.

Jake looked across at him.

'The offer still stands with you, Neville. You can go if you want. You've done more than enough already.'

Neville shook his head slowly and sighed.

'Nope. I guess if I ever get the chance to write this up for the *Chronicle*, I ain't going to get much closer to the action than this, am I?'

Jake smiled. He handed the rifle to Elaine and told her to go over to the cell door.

'Cover Nate with this. Carter's a gambling man. He knows we're holding the ace.'

Elaine nodded. She went over to the cell and placed the rifle through the bars, pointing at Nate's chest. He lay still drugged on his bunk, a small smile on his young lips, obviously dreaming about happier times. Elaine couldn't help but think how innocent he looked. She wondered when in his young life he had become so cruel.

The group of men outside was now gathered round the hitching rail just at the bottom of the steps of the boardwalk. There was a murmur of conversation. Suddenly Carter's voice cut through the night.

'Chalmers! Chalmers! I want a word with you. You can come out and talk with us,' shouted Carter. 'I don't want anyone getting hurt. I want to deal with this with as little bloodshed as possible.'

Jake opened the front door and stepped out on to the boardwalk. Neville followed behind him.

'If this is about getting your brother back, you're wasting your time. He's goin' to stand trial. If anything happens to me or any of the people in here, there's a gun pointing straight at Nate.'

'Well, I've got an idea, Chalmers.

Give us Nate. Let us look after him until the judge gets here. We'll make sure he gets a fair trial. You know I want to see justice done as much as you.'

Jake stared at him.

'I've seen your type of justice. You're a strange man to be talking about high-falutin things like fairness and justice. Within a few hours you'd have him heading towards Arizona and across the border where nobody could touch him. You could afford to set him up there for years. No deal, Carter. He stays here. In my jail.' Both men realized that Jake had said the word '*my*'.

Carter stared at the toe of his highly shined black boots as though annoyed at the rime of dust dirtying them. After a moment he looked up. He hid his anger well.

'You're a big disappointment, Chalmers. Don't say I didn't try and help you out of this mess.' He seemed to think for a minute, then said, 'but I'll tell you what. Here's another offer. You've got until daybreak to get out of this town. We were doing just fine here until you turned up and started poking your nose into our business. Your interfering got Luke killed. Nate may have pulled the trigger but you filled Luke's head with ideas that were way too high above his station. He was out of his league. You made him think he could take me on. That was a big mistake. You think about that every time you look in the shaving mirror and see Luke Gardner staring back out at you.'

'I didn't kill Luke Gardner. The boy stays with me,' said Jake.

'Well, the deal still stands. I'm a reasonable man but you're pushing me too far. If you don't hand him over in twelve hours, I'm coming back to get him.'

'Is that a threat?'

'You take it any way you like. Take it as a promise. I'm gonna come down here and pull this jailhouse down brick by brick, plank by plank until I get my brother back. You've got some time to think about that.'

He looked over Jake's shoulder and raised his voice slightly.

'And that goes for anyone else who decides to stand in my way.'

Jake turned to go back into the jail, but Neville stood transfixed with a gaunt, white expression on his face.

'What's wrong, Neville?' asked Jake, although he had seen fear often enough in men's eyes to recognize it. Neville started to lower the gun, his hands were trembling, his month dry and sickly.

'Jake . . . you know . . . I'm not a fighter. I don't have the stomach for this. I don't fight like this. I fight with my pen. I don't use bullets. I use words. I'm no good to you here.'

Jake nodded, smiled and put a hand on his friend's shoulder reassuringly. 'I don't blame you, Neville. If you're not used to this type of thing, it gets pretty grating on the nerves. I understand.'

'It's not like I'm running out on you, Jake, I really believe in what you're doing here. Making this stand against

Carter and his men, but — '

'Forget it, Neville. You don't have to explain. I'm surprised you stuck around this long. You've been a good friend to me.'

Jake put his hand out and Neville took it nervously. He offered Jake the gun, then slowly stepped off the stoop and headed towards his newspaper office. Carter stuck his thumbs into the front of this belt and smiled broadly as he watched Neville go.

'See that, Jake? There's only you and a slip of a girl who's young enough to be impressed with cheap heroics. Against these men? You don't stand a chance.'

'Maybe,' conceded Jake, tapping the silver sheriff's badge, 'but maybe I'm too dumb or too old-fashioned to think that what this represents is worth fighting for and it's more powerful than anything you can do.'

Carter scowled.

'How many times I gotta tell you, Chalmers? I'm the law around here.

I've told you before but you're so pig-headed you keep wanting to find out the hard way. Well, that's up to you. We'll see just what kind of justice my boys dispense when we come back around here again tomorrow morning.'

He turned on his heel and pushed his way through the group of men standing stony-faced behind him. Then they too turned and followed him up the main street towards the Eldorado. Jake watched them go, then turned inside the jailhouse for what he knew was going to be a very long night.

Elaine was still standing at the cell doors, the gun trained on Nate.

'Where's Neville?' she asked, looking behind Jake.

'He's gone,' said Jake simply. No recrimination. No blame. 'There's still time for you to get out too.'

Elaine bit her bottom lip, then pulled the gun from between the bars.

'I reckon I'm too involved now to pull out. I guess you're stuck with me.'

Jake smiled, and for the first time it

was a warm smile.

'Want some coffee?' she asked.

Jake nodded and moved back over to the window to take up his watch.

'He says we've got until daybreak. I've no doubt he'll keep his word. So we got the night to come up with a plan of how we're gonna ride this thing out until the judge gets here.

'Why until daybreak? I mean, why not rush us now? There's only two of us.'

'He'll want to wear us down. Be seen to be giving us a chance. He'll give us time to be hungry and thirsty. He'll let us stew here and let things go through our minds. Things like dying. He knows we're not going anywhere so we got plenty of time to consider our options.'

'The circuit-riding judge might not be around for a few days. D'you think we can hold out that long?'

'I don't know, Elaine. I don't know,' said Jake, turning back to the window. 'I really don't know.'

Elaine started to check through the

cupboards. There were a few tins — not many but enough to keep the hunger pangs at bay for a while.

'Luke ate out at the saloon most days,' explained Jake when he saw the meagre rations.

'Looks like we're living on coffee then.' Elaine laughed.

She lifted the coffee pot from the stove and opened the rear door to fill it with water from the pump in the yard. Jake turned around and saw her just in time to leap across the room.

'No, Elaine!' he screamed as a single shot ricocheted off the doorframe. She fell back into the room, the coffee pot clanging on the floor. Jake ran across, slammed the door shut and helped her to her feet. She was white and shaking.

'Are you all right?' he asked, checking for any sign of injury or bleeding.

She nodded, taking deep shuddering breaths. A peal of high-pitched boyish laughter rang out. Nate, his face pressed to the steel bars of his cage, was convulsed in laughter.

'You're trapped as sure as mice in a gin trap. I reckon there's not much time left for you two. If you want to save your hides — and you have got such a pretty hide, darlin' — you'll let me go.'

Jake ignored him as he slid the bolt back on the door.

'No food or water for us means nothing for you either.'

Nate grinned broadly as he went back to his bunk still chortling. He lay stretched out and gazed up at the roof.

'I'll survive. I got my future to look forward to. What have you two got?'

18

Neville Chuster let himself quietly into the darkened newspaper office. The moonlight shone through the front windows and lit the black shining machinery lying dormant in the dark. He locked the door behind him and pulled down the blinds. He wanted to hide from the world for a while, even though he knew he had done the right thing. He would have been no good to Jake; just somebody else whom he would have had to protect.

Elaine was better with a gun than he was and Neville knew himself well enough to know that when it came down to it, he couldn't have taken the life of another human being.

My gun is my pen. Words are my bullets.

The words spun around his head. Yes, he was good at words. Always had been, but now the power of those words had deserted him. Jake didn't need words. He needed action. Fighting men didn't talk much. He slammed his hand on the desk in frustration. He had never felt so ashamed of himself. His head pounded and there was a sickness in the pit of his stomach when he thought about how he had left those two young people to their fate.

He suddenly felt so, so tired. These last few days had taken a heavy toll from him. He sat on the high stool in front of the line print and lowered his head on to the wide metallic slab. The cool of the metal helped soothe his pounding head. His fingers reached out and felt the roughness of the upturned type. And in his head, the words that he had spoken to Jake Chalmers as he left his side kept reverberating in his mind.

He was almost slipping off to sleep when a sharp rap at the window made him spin round. He slid off the stool and, crouching low, walked over to his desk, his heart pounding. Was this

Carter's men coming for him? He knew there would be repercussions but hadn't thought it would happen so soon. Again, he felt the bitter taste of fear. The door was rapped again but this time, he heard a voice he thought he recognized.

'Chuster?' came a loud whisper. 'You there?'

Neville pulled open the top drawer of his desk and pulled out his old Colt Navy .36. Fumbling with clumsy hands, he broke it open and checked that each chamber had a bullet. He'd never used it before — he didn't even know whether it would work. Then, his hands shaking, he walked over to the door. He put his hand on the door handle and listened. He could hear the low pant of tortured breathing. Then the voice again.

'Chuster . . . Chuster . . . help . . . me . . . '

Neville pulled open the door quickly, thrusting out his gun as he did so.

Jeremiah Isaacs, his face drenched

with blood stood wobbling in front of him. Then he fell forward so suddenly that Neville had to catch him with both hands. With a great effort he dragged him into the office and closed the door quickly behind them. He brought the kerosene lamp over from his desk and lit it. As the light slowly rose, Neville was shocked to see the state of the wounded man lying on his floor. Blood had run from his head and dried in his hair and on his face leaving a hideous mask down one side. His cheek was badly gashed and blood ran from an open wound. Terrible swelling around his eyes prevented him from opening them and his clothes were torn and tattered.

'Jeremiah? Jeremiah?' said Neville. 'What in the Lord's name has happened to you?'

Jeremiah managed to open his eyes a little. Through dried and cracked lips he managed to utter some words.

'You were right . . . about Carter. We've got to . . . stop him.'

His eyes closed again and Neville thought he'd fainted.

Neville put a pan of water to heat on the stove and turned up the lamp. He poured some whiskey into a small glass, and holding his head, got him to swallow a little. Jeremiah stirred and with a lot of effort, Neville helped him on to his feet and got him on to a chair beside his desk. He heated a small pan of water and started the task of cleaning and bandaging his wounds. It was almost midnight before Jeremiah was strong enough to sit up in his chair and tell him the full story of what had happened.

It was almost another two hours before they had decided what they were going to do.

19

The sun had not been in the sky for long. Although it shone brightly, the cool of the night still lingered. Most of the town had still to wake up, but Jordan Carter had not slept. He had kept a lonely vigil throughout the night, nursing a slow burning fury and waited for daylight. Since the first break of dawn he and his men had been busy and now he stood in the middle of the street and surveyed their work. He turned and looked up towards the jailhouse.

'OK, Jake,' he shouted, 'it's all over. Time to come out. Bring Nate and the girl with you.'

His voice broke through the heavy silence of the morning and echoed along the length of the deserted main street. Behind him, ten of his men held rifles to their eyes behind their roughly erected barricade of barrels, crates and an overturned wagon, which stretched across the street.

He waited patiently for Jake to reply. He was just about to raise his voice again when he saw the blind behind the barred window rise a little and Jake's clear and determined voice cut through the dawn air.

'Can't do that, Carter. I ain't comin' out and you're sure not comin' in.'

There was a pause as Jake's voice travelled the length of the street, then faded into an uneasy silence. Then Carter spoke again.

'You're backing me into a corner, Chalmers. I don't want this to end in bloodshed but you're leaving me little choice.'

'I'm staying here 'til the district judge comes in.'

Carter shook his head; a wry smile cracked his face.

'It's not going to happen, Chalmers. You're never going to see him. You may as well give up now.'

There was no reply.

The men behind the barricade suddenly looked up as a pigeon took to the sky and somewhere in the distance a dog barked. Other than that, the street was eerily quiet. When there was no further response, Carter started to walk towards the jailhouse, calling out as he went.

'I told you I would be prepared to take this jail down, nail by nail, brick by brick. You know I ain't bluffin', Chalmers. You could save a lot of blood being spilled today.'

Suddenly Jake shoved the barrel of the rifle through the bottom left-hand pane of the jailhouse window. Carter hesitated at the sound of shattering glass, then kept walking towards the building, but he stopped abruptly when a .36 calibre slug buried itself in the dirt not two inches from his boot.

'I'm good at carrying out threats too, Carter.'

Jordan stared at the hole in the dust for a moment, then slowly looked up towards the office.

'Well, it looks to me as though you've made your decision.'

He turned and walked quickly back towards the barricade, signalling to the men as he did so to take their positions. Obediently, they arranged themselves solidly behind the wall, rifles sticking out like black spikes, leaving no target for Jake to hit.

Jake saw what was about to happen. He ran across the room and grabbed Luke's solid oak desk. He tipped it over and pulled it on to its side, grunting with the effort. He roughly grabbed Elaine and shoved her down behind it.

'Keep your head down, Elaine. Things are going to get a bit noisy around here.'

He jumped up and ran over to the window. He had barely reached the stone alcove when what seemed like an explosion burst through the windows. Eleven repeating Winchester rifles let off their vicious salvoes in rapid succession. The very walls seemed to shake from the ferocious volleys that battered relentlessly against the front of the building.

It seemed to go on for ever. Faced with overwhelming firepower, Jake did not get the opportunity to fire off one shot in retaliation. He strained to look through the dust-filled room towards the desk and although he couldn't see her, he could hear Elaine whimper and cry in fear as bullets embedded themselves in the desk. At least he knew she was alive. The desk seemed to be holding, although large slivers of wood were slicing off as bullets came through the window and found their way across the room.

Even the solid oak front door was beginning to disintegrate slowly under the barrage. Small golden arrows of morning sunlight were beginning to spike through the holes. The guns crashed painfully in their ears and the acrid smell of gunpowder smoke burned their throats and made their eyes water.

Then, as suddenly as it had begun, the gunfire stopped. The silence that replaced the deafening noise was almost as painful on their battered eardrums. Jake immediately swung into position at the window and let off a few rounds to discourage anyone making a run through the front. But Carter knew he had the advantage. He didn't have to do anything risky.

'Had enough, Chalmers?' shouted Carter from behind the barricade.

'We're doing just fine,' lied Jake.

'I'm warning you. If we start again we ain't gonna stop until I walk through those doors. You can't hold out for ever!'

'First one over the door gets a lead welcome.'

A single shot ricocheted against the iron bars on the window. Jake jumped back, yelling at Elaine to keep her head down.

'OK, boys, let them have it.'

The deadly rain of bullets began again. Pressed flat against the wall, he knew they couldn't survive this siege for much longer. It was only a matter of time before a stray bullet got them. The door and windows and even the adobe walls wouldn't hold out for ever. Jake felt helplessly pinned down. Frantically his mind raced as he tried to think of a way out of this trap.

Then, suddenly soaring above the din came a scream. The gunfire slowly subsided as every man wondered whether it had been a man or a beast that the unearthly scream had come from. It was human. It came from the cell. Jake and Elaine peered through the dust and could make out Nate, rolling hysterically on the cell floor, clutching his right arm. Dark blood was coursing through his fingers and spreading on the dusty, brick floor.

'They got me,' he was screaming. 'Sweet Jesus, they got me — my arm — I . . . I think I've lost my arm.'

Throwing caution aside, Elaine jumped up from behind the desk before Jake could do anything to stop her.

'Elaine! Don't!' he yelled.

'Can't you see he's hurt bad?' she shouted as she ran to the jailhouse. She grabbed the keys from the hook on the doorframe and before Jake could get to her she had swung open the heavy door and was inside the cell, kneeling over Nate with concern etched on her face, pulling his hand away, almost dreading to see the terrible wounds that were causing the boy so much pain.

Nate continued to roll around the ground until she was kneeling beside him. Then, before they knew what was happening, he had grabbed her around the throat in a vicelike arm lock so tight her face suddenly turned crimson. Jake ran into the cell.

'Get back!' Nate screamed at him, 'get back or I swear I'll throttle her like a turkey at Thanksgiving. I swear it!'

He was sweating and panting but grinning wildly at his deceit.

'Your arm . . . ' began Jake.

'Oldest trick in the book. Just unpicked the bandage in my hand. I ain't shot. I ain't even hurt — but Lord, you're going to be hurtin' so soon. Drop the gun!'

Jake hesitated.

'Drop it, ya sonofabitch. I swear to God I'll break her pretty little neck right here and now!'

His grip tightened with a vicious tug to prove there was no doubt he would carry through his threat. Jake reluctantly let the gun drop to the floor. Elaine was whimpering with fear, tears rolling down her face. Saliva started to drip from her chin as she found it harder and harder to swallow.

'You're going to strangle her. Let her go.'

Nate shook his head fiercely and grinned like a madman.

'This ain't nothing to what I'm going to do to her once you're out of the way, Mr Lawman.' He smiled widely, showing straight, white teeth. 'Oh my, you are goin' to be so sorry you messed with my brother and me. Now keep your hands where I can see 'em and kick the gun over to me.'

Jake raised his hands to the height of his shoulder and then carefully kicked his Colt. It glided across the dusty floor and came to rest next to Nate's good hand. He grabbed it, cocked it and pointed it levelly at Jake's chest.

He struggled to his feet but kept his grip tightly around Elaine's neck. When stood up he grabbed one of her arms and twisted it roughly up behind her back. She winced in pain and stared into Jake's eyes with wide-eyed fear, but she couldn't say anything. Nate sidled over to the nearest window, dragging Elaine with him, never once taking his eyes or his gun from Jake. He lifted the butt of the gun and smashed the window, then shouted out through the broken glass.

'Jordan? Jordan? You out there?'

'Nate. That you?' came back Jordan's unmistakable voice.

'Jordan! Get in here! I got the girl. I got the gun off Chalmers. Get in here.' Within minutes, Jordan and some of his men ran in through the badly shot-up front door. He quickly surveyed the situation and grinned widely.

'Well done, Nate. Well done.'

Jordan walked over to Jake. He stopped in front of him. They were of equal height and their eyes looked levelly into each other's. Carter stared at Jake with undisguised hatred.

'Well, well, Mr Chalmers, it seems that law and order have finally been restored to Sweetwater,' said Carter coldly.

His eyes drifted down to take in the silver badge in Jake's lapel. He put his hand up to it, fingering it, admiring it then suddenly pulled it fiercely from Jake's vest, ripping the leather as he did so. He gazed at it nestling in the palm of his hand, as though estimating its weight, then slowly and deliberately pinned it on to the lapel of his own coat. He smiled broadly, turning round so his men could admire the shiny badge. They grinned and congratulated him. Carter turned to face Jake again.

He grabbed each of his lapels with his hands and, in a mock solemn voice, began to announce, 'I, Mr Jordan Carter, am hereby officially in charge of Sweetwater. That means, Mr Chalmers, that I am sheriff, judge and jury. And so, with the powers that I have invested in myself, I hereby find you guilty of murder and kidnapping, the punishment for which means that you will be taken from this place and hanged by the neck until you are dead.'

Then, without warning, he brought his right hand down swiftly into a fist and buried it deep into Jake's midriff, knocking the air from his lungs. Elaine let out a scream as Jake sank to his knees with a groan. Then Carter raised the butt of his pistol and whipped it fiercely across the back of Jake's head. Jake passed out into oblivion, curled like a baby on the floor as blood seeped from a deep wound and dyed his hair jet-black.

'No, Jake, no . . . ' screamed Elaine, then broke into sobs as Nate continued to hold her back.

Carter turned round to the group of men who gathered around Jake's unconscious form.

'Gentlemen, take this man and do what you have to do. I think we have unfinished business to attend to. May God have mercy on his soul.'

He started laughing and the other men joined in as they lifted Jake and dragged him out into the street. Outside, a noose had already been prepared and it was already swinging in the hot sun from a supporting gantry. The other end of the rope was tied around the pommel of a nearby horse.

Carter gazed up the deserted street, then raised his voice.

'Let it be known that this is what happens when you try to cross the Carter brothers! Let this be a warning to you all!'

For the second time, a hanging rope was roughly slid around Jake's neck and he was pushed up on to the horse's haunches, still barely conscious. Elaine cried out to him but Nate held her tight, his bloody hand over her mouth.

The horse was jittery and nervous, perhaps sensing the approach of death. It pawed the ground and showed the whites of its eyes as one of Carter's men did his best to hold it still. Carter watched it for a moment and then turned to Nate.

'Nate? D'you want the honour?'

'Yes sirree! I sure do!' cried Nate.

He pushed Elaine into the arms of two of the gang who were standing next to her, then jumped down from the boardwalk and stood alongside the horse.

'Make sure she watches this,' he shouted to Elaine's captors.

He looked up at Jake, whose eyes were glazing over as he fought to stay conscious.

'So long, Mr Lawman,' Nate sneered. He raised his hand above the horse's flank. A wicked grin stretched across his face then he froze. A single rifle shot had rung out and now small spurts of deep-red blood were starting to flow out of the small bullet hole in the back of his neck. Like a falling tree, he slowly fell backwards on to the sand and lay still just as the echo of the gunshot died away.

Then all hell broke loose as men dived for cover. The horse reared and pulled its reins from the helpless gunman, who tried in vain to control it. It lunged forward, wide-eyed with fear, oblivious to the weight on its back. It reared on to its hind legs, screaming in terror, pawing the air in its need to get away. Jake gently slid from its back as the horse shot forward and galloped up Main Street, unsure of where to run.

As the horse ran, Jake was left suspended two feet from the ground, his boots desperately grabbing at the sand. Elaine broke from the two bruisers as they ran for cover. She reached Jake, almost banging into Neville, who had suddenly appeared beside him. He handed Elaine a knife and, as he wrapped his arms around

Jake's waist and took the weight from the rope, Elaine reached up and cut the rope, sending Jake and Neville bundling to the ground like two bales of hay. Elaine leapt down beside him, cradled his blood-streaked head on her lap and stroked his hair away from his eyes.

'Jake — Jake speak to me, Jake. It's me, Elaine.'

His eyes flicked open and he swallowed painfully. He whispered something.

'What did you say, Jake? I can't hear you.'

He raised his voice a little higher. 'That was close . . . ' was all he said.

Along both sides of the boardwalk, out of houses, alleyways and shops, the townsfolk of Sweetwater emerged with guns covering all of Carter's men. Jeremiah Isaacs, his face bruised and swollen, and limping badly walked up to Jordan Carter.

'Tell your men to drop their guns. It's all over, Carter. You're outmanned and outgunned. Neville was right. I was wrong,' said Jeremiah. 'This town doesn't belong to you. It belongs to us. The people. You're not the law, we are.'

Carter stared at him with undiluted hatred as, around him, his men came out with their hands up and their guns softly thudded to the ground. He looked around and saw his kid brother sprawled lifeless in the dust.

'Who are these people?' he spat.

'These,' said Jeremiah, 'are the 1st Sweetwater Militia. Neville and I rounded them up last night. Volunteers to a man and prepared to lay down their lives to stop crooks like you from taking over their town.'

Carter glared at them as his men were herded past him by a group of determined militiamen.

'Time you joined your men behind bars, Carter.'

As Jeremiah took Carter by the arm to follow his men, Jake got up from the dust and walked unsteadily over to him. The two men faced each other, eye to eye. They stayed that way for what seemed an age, then Jake raised his hand slowly. He put his fingers around the silver badge that still rested on Carter's lapel and tugged swiftly. The expensive cloth ripped easily.

'Well, well, Mr Carter, it seems that law and order have now been restored to Sweetwater. Lock him up, Mr Isaacs.'

Jake turned around and started walking towards Elaine. Jeremiah smiled broadly and saluted.

'Sure thing, Sheriff.'

As Jeremiah went to take his prisoner by the arm, Carter quickly reached into the back of his shirt and pulled out a slim pearl-handled stiletto blade. It flashed in the sunlight before slashing down quickly. With a groan, Jeremiah fell backwards clutching his forearm as blood oozed from a deep wound below his shirtsleeve.

As men went to help Jeremiah, Carter saw his chance and sprinted towards the horse that had been tethered nearby. He leapt into the saddle. It reared on its hind legs and let out a frightened neigh. In the confusion a few shots rang out but before anyone could grab the horse, Carter was fiercely spurring it towards the far end of town.

'Quick, Elaine — help me saddle up Paulo!'

They both ran to the livery stable, Jake grabbing a Winchester rifle from one of the militiamen as he went.

In the stall, Jake threw the saddle on Paulo's back and Elaine tightened up the girth straps. Jake shoved the rifle into the sheath as Elaine slipped on the halter and bit and handed the reins to Jake, who had already swung himself up into the saddle.

Within five minutes, Jake had ridden out of the livery stable, out of the yard and was galloping up the street, cheered on by the group of bystanders.

'Be careful, Jake,' called out Elaine but her words were lost in a cloud of dust as Jake spurred Paulo after Carter.

20

It didn't take long before Jake and Paulo were clear of the town boundary. Even with the start that Carter had, Jake could already see him up ahead in the distance.

Carter might have been an ace poker-player but he was no horseman. Clumsy in the saddle and with an unfamiliar mount, he soon lost ground to the close working partnership of Jake and Paulo. Fluid and balanced in the saddle, Jake sat slightly forward away from the cantle and used the rowels on his spurs sparingly. He knew he didn't have to ask much from Paulo who would have run until his heart burst.

Carter had a hunch he would be pursued, but when he looked over his shoulder, he didn't expect to see the earnest figure of Jake in pursuit and closing the gap with each passing minute. Quickly, Carter decided it was futile to try and outrun him in a straight race. His best bet was to head for cover. He wheeled the horse roughly over to the west and headed for the foothills from where, only a few days ago, Jake had come.

Soon the ground-cover changed. The flat dusty plain soon became shale-covered, with large, sharp rocks scattered around. This was no terrain to gallop over, especially for an inexperienced rider with a strange horse, but Carter, as usual, was prepared to take the risk. The stakes were high. He had a whole town riding on the outcome of what he knew would be his final encounter with Jake Chalmers.

Jake watched Carter's change of tactics and cursed the reckless stupidity of the man. As the ground cover changed, he started to pull back gently on the reins and let Paulo pick his own way through the treacherous rock-strewn terrain. He knew he could keep Carter in view without breaking his or his horse's neck.

The ground slowly became steeper and the rocky outcrops grew larger. Jake knew what Carter was up to. He was heading for cover, probably to hole up for a while and then to try and give him the slip under the cover of darkness. Either that or it was to lie in wait for him and ambush him as Jake tried to follow him into the hills.

Jake watched grimly as Carter whipped his horse fiercely with the loose reins as it plunged and reared up the rocky slopes, trying to keep its balance in the uncertain terrain.

Suddenly, they disappeared from sight behind a large rock fall. Jake pulled Paulo to a halt and slowly slid to the ground. After tethering his reins to a nearby bush he came to Paulo's side and pulled out the Winchester rifle. He rubbed Paulo's mane.

'You stay here, boy. It's too dangerous for you. I'll see you if I get back.' As he started to make his way up on foot, Jake realized he'd used the words, '*if* I get back'.

He put the thought out of his head and started to make his way carefully up the rock-strewn hill. On foot, he knew he could make less noise and actually make faster headway. As he made progress up the hill, with the sun now beating down on him, he weighed up the situation. Carter had the advantage in that he was up above him and he could easily hide whereas Jake had to try and flush him out. But Jake was more used to operating in this sort of terrain and he had a gun. Carter might have a derringer slipped up his sleeve but that was no good except at close range. Jake stopped to check that the rifle was fully loaded and considered that the Winchester might not be the great advantage it seemed. Certainly, if Carter was careless and exposed himself long enough for him to get a clear shot Jake was sure he wouldn't miss the opportunity, but he knew Carter wouldn't let that happen. Jake suspected that Carter still had the stiletto. He had shown he wasn't frightened of using it. All things considered, Carter's main edge was the element of surprise. He knew he just had to sit tight. Jake had to go in and get him.

Jake moved swiftly but quietly up the side of the hills. Every now and again he stopped and, once his breath had slowed and his heart beat stopped pounding in his ears, he could occasionally hear the rumbling clatter of shale as Carter, still mounted, spurred his beast on up the hillside.

Jake knew the horse wouldn't be able to keep that up for much longer. Sure enough, a few minutes later, Jake heard the horse's terrified scream shatter the stillness. Jake knew it had slipped. It had only been a matter of time. It was difficult to pinpoint exactly where the cry had come from, but Jake hurried in its general direction.

A few minutes later Jake found the horse. It was on its side, thrashing the stony ground with three legs, its fourth front leg painfully jammed in a wedge of rock up which no sane horseman would have attempted to go. Its eyes were wild with fear and pain, its flank was sweat-soaked and its mouth covered in foam. The leg was clearly broken and the beast would never get up again. Carter had left it to die. Jake raised the Winchester to the horse's head. The single gunshot echoed round the hills and Jake ruefully wondered whether Carter had made him give his position away on purpose.

The sun was now beating down mercilessly. The powder-dry rocks and large, flat-sided boulders reflected the heat, so that the hills became an oven.

He moved as quickly as he could but now, from round every boulder and over every summit he expected an attack at any time. The rifle was slippery with sweat in his hands and he had to repeatedly stop and wipe his palms against his dirty pants to stop it sliding out of his hands altogether.

Eventually, he rested against a large, vertical rock face and leaned the rifle up against the wall. He wiped his brow with the back of his dirty sleeve, then rested his head against the rock and closed his eyes. The sound of metal against stone made him jump. Looking down, he saw the rifle sliding sideways. He reached down to grab it just as a large boulder crashed on to the rock where just a second ago his head had been resting.

Carter scrambled away on the rocks above and Jake leapt after him, following the sound of scrabbling boots. With his hands and boots slipping on smooth rock, he somehow managed to climb up the sheer face. Eventually, with nails broken and hands bleeding, he heaved himself up on the top of a large flat rock. At the other end, Carter was waiting for him.

He looked dirty and dishevelled; no longer the smooth, sophisticated gambler, but a lean, desperate killer. His black hair was yellowed with dust and sweat had made long streaks in the dirt on his face. Standing in the sun, his legs apart, Jake could see the toll the last few hours had taken on him, His expensive pants were torn and dirt-streaked. He had got rid of his jacket and his shirtsleeves were ripped but, beyond his tattered exterior, there was still the determined glint in his eyes of a man who was not used to losing and was not about to start now. In his hand, glinting in the sun, he slowly turned the deadly stiletto blade. He beckoned Jake to approach.

'It's just you and me now, Chalmers,' he said though gritted teeth. 'Only one of us is going to walk away from this.'

Jake walked slowly towards him. Carter watched him like a wounded animal. When they were barely six feet apart, without warning Carter lunged forward. Jake jumped to the side, his boot nearly slipping on the edge of the flat rock on which they were both standing. Carter was smiling now. An ugly, evil grin. He lunged forward again with a wide, swiping movement. As Jake jumped aside the blade caught the front of his shirt, the edge so sharp it sliced through the material cleanly. Jake reached down and felt the warm dampness of blood on his chest.

'Come on, Mr Lawman,' jeered Carter. 'There's more where that came from . . . '

Bolstered now, having drawn first blood, Carter started lunging repeatedly, sometimes stabbing, sometimes slashing, deadly intent etched on his face. Jake quickly unbuckled his empty gunbelt and wished, not for the first time, that he had taken just a few minutes to retrieve his Colt before leaving town. He wrapped the tanned leather strip around his hand and swept the buckle side in front of him to keep Carter away. Carter was smiling now, sure that if he just waited for the right moment, victory would be his.

As Carter lunged forward again Jake used the belt like a whip, wrapping it round his wrist. He yanked hard, pulling Carter off his feet. Carter sprawled to the ground, the deadly blade slipping from his hand. Both men made a desperate lunge for it, but Jake managed to get to it first. He pushed it out of the way, then hauled Carter to his feet and turned him around to face him. With the last of his strength he smashed his fist into Carter's jaw, sending him reeling backwards to lie still in the dust. Jake stood over him, poised to slug it out if Carter rose to his feet again — but Carter lay still.

Jake took a few steps backwards and sank to his knees. He felt drained and exhausted. Panting heavily, he lifted the knife out of the dust and stared at it. With his back to Carter, he looked over the edge of the rock, wiping sweat from his eyes and tried to get his breath back.

Suddenly, the bright sun above him was blacked out as a shadow passed. Jake instinctively whirled round and thrust his hand out to protect himself. The knife was still in his hand and it buried itself up to the hilt deep into Carter's chest. Carter stood with a rock above his head, then he let it slip from his fingers, staggering backwards. Jake let the handle of the knife go and felt the sticky redness of blood.

Carter stumbled backwards clutching his chest in pain. Disbelief clouded his eyes. Then, taking another two steps, he lost his balance and disappeared over the side of the rocky ledge without a sound.

21

Three months after the death of Jordan Carter, Jake stepped out on to the boardwalk outside the sheriff's office. The sun was sinking, turning the vast blue sky above the town of Sweetwater to shades of yellow and orange. He looked up. It was going to be a beautiful sunset.

The main street was as busy as on the first day that Jake had ridden in from the hills; a dust-covered drifter no more likely to put down roots than a wind-tossed piece of tumbleweed. Now, nearly three months later, it felt like a different place. Gone were the suspicion and fear in people's eyes, gone the constant threat of trouble just around the corner. Jake couldn't help but give a little smile to himself. He would never have believed it would give him such a warm glow to watch ordinary people going about their lawful business, and kids playing safely in the street.

Straightening the silver badge on his vest, the way Luke Gardener used to, he slowly closed the sheriff's office door behind him and started to make his way to the church hall which doubled as the local schoolhouse and where the monthly town council meetings were held.

People acknowledged him as he passed. He touched the brim of his new black Stetson with the edge of a forefinger and returned their warm smiles. He was still getting used to being a somebody after spending most of his life being no one.

After a hundred yards or so he heard light footsteps behind him. Before he could turn round he felt a slim arm slip through his. He looked down at Elaine's smiling face as she hugged him close.

'Mind if I tag along?' she asked, almost skipping along beside him.

'Sure. Don't mind if you do. Just to

the next corner though, I'm picking up another pretty girl there.'

'Oh, you . . . ' she laughed and punched his arm playfully.

'Hey — you could get in trouble for that. I think that constitutes an assault on a federal officer.'

'Well, listen to you, Mr Sheriff. It seems all that book-learning with Neville is paying off.'

Jake felt himself go a little red. For the last few months he'd spent almost every evening studying hard with Neville and even though he still found it hard work, he was making good progress. Neville was a good teacher and Jake was bright and keen to learn.

This was just one of the many good things that had happened to him since that day he'd ridden back to town with the broken body of Jordan Carter slung over Paulo's back. As his exhausted horse had slowly walked into the main street, he found that Jeremiah Isaacs had taken charge and all of Carter's henchmen had been rounded up and locked in the jail. Once the townsfolk of Sweetwater were back in charge, things started happening and, like a living thing, the town started slowly to heal itself.

A few days later Judge Grady, the circuit-riding judge arrived. The schoolhouse was quickly converted into a court room and he wasted no time in putting Carter's men on trial. Their cases were heard swiftly but to the letter of the law. There was no shortage of witnesses and the twelve-man jury found them guilty of all charges brought against them. They were duly sentenced to various lengths of hard labour in the frontier prison.

The second thing Judge Grady did was to have Jake officially sworn in as acting sheriff of Sweetwater on the two provisions that he was answerable to the mayor (once one was elected) and that he learned to read and write in order to carry out his duties properly. Judge Grady had told him he would be back in three or four months' time and he would be testing Jake on points of law.

Within a month Neville had organized the town's first proper election. There were three candidates but it was always a foregone conclusion and Jeremiah Isaacs, easily the most popular choice, was duly sworn in as Sweetwater's first mayor. The first thing the new mayor did was to select Neville Chuster as chairman of the town council, and his decision was supported unanimously. With the Carter brothers dead, their property and businesses were sold off to reputable local businessmen; this time, however, the way they operated those businesses was closely controlled and licensed by the town council, which had the power to close any business down that was in breach of local laws.

Looking back on everything that had happened in such a short time, sometimes Jake had to pinch himself in case he was dreaming. He just couldn't believe he was a sheriff of a law-abiding town, with his beautiful fiancée on his arm and on his way to address his first meeting of the local town council.

'I'm not looking forward to this,' he said quietly to Elaine. 'I ain't never made a speech before.'

'You'll be fine. Everybody's rooting for you.'

When they eventually arrived at the church hall, there was a small gathering of people outside, but when they saw the sheriff approach they hastily made their way into the building. Inside, a long table had been set up against the back wall. Facing it were rows of chairs filled with townspeople who looked round expectantly when their new sheriff appeared in the doorway. Jake stopped when he saw that all eyes were on him. If Elaine hadn't had a good grip on his arm he might have turned round and headed back to the safety of his office. Elaine squeezed his arm and smiled up at him.

'Go on, Sheriff. They're all waiting to hear what you got to say.'

Jake cleared his throat and made his way to the top table. He sat down beside Jeremiah Isaacs, who was resplendent in a new frock-coat and top hat. On his other side was Neville Chuster who smiled broadly at Jake, patted his shoulder and nodded encouragement.

After a few minutes Neville rose to his feet, picked up the small gavel that was in front of him and banged the table for order. The buzz of conversation faded to silence. The chairman cleared his throat noisily.

'Well, good evening, good citizens of Sweetwater. Welcome to the monthly meeting of the Sweetwater town council. I'll be going through a few things that I have on the agenda for this evening's meeting, but first I'd like you to welcome a man who needs no introduction: our newly elected town sheriff, Jake Chalmers.'

Jake blushed as a spontaneous round of applause spread around the room, started, he suspected, by Elaine, who beamed at him from the back of the room.

'Welcome, Sheriff. I believe you have a few words you'd like to say.'

Jake rose uncertainly to his feet as Neville took his seat.

'Evenin', folks,' he said quietly. 'As you all probably know, I ain't too good with words — at least not as good as these two gentlemen here,' the crowd laughed a little, 'but I'll do my best. This won't take long.'

He went into the top pocket of his vest beside the silver badge and took out a little slip of paper which he gently unfolded.

'First, I'd just like to say how grateful I am that you thought me fit to be your sheriff. It's a real honour and a privilege and I promise to do the best I can. Just like Luke Gardner would have wanted me to do.'

A murmur of approval buzzed around the room.

'And the other thing is something I want to see changed in the running of the town. It's only an idea and Jeremiah and Neville — I mean, the mayor and the chairman — well, they don't know anything about this and if they don't agree, well I guess I'll just have to save it for another day.'

He looked around at the two men, who nodded their encouragement for him to continue, eager to know what it was he was going to suggest.

'Not a lot of people know this, but when I was a kid, I lost my ma and pa to two drunken gunslingers who gunned them down in the street. I know some of you here have suffered similar losses, too.'

He looked up quickly and saw Elaine. Her eyes were bright with tears. Abe McDonnell, sitting in the front row, nodded his head.

'I don't have to tell you people about the trouble we had in this town with gunslingers and their like. Well, before he died, my pa always told me that he thought there would come a day when we could run our lives and our towns and protect our families and our property with the law. He dreamed of a time when it would be the law of the people and not the law of the gun that people would have a healthy respect for, but I guess I was too young to understand. I never believed him and I never thought that I would see that day. So, what I'm getting to . . . what I'd like to say to the town council is that we pass a law in Sweetwater that says everyone has to hand in their guns when they enter the town limits. They give them to me. I'll keep them safely locked away and they can pick 'em up again when they leave. That should make sure that we don't get drunken brawls turning into gunfights and innocent people getting hurt or killed. I reckon from now we can sort out anything we need to in a meeting or a courtroom. Not in the street.'

There was a lot of nodding heads and approval in the room. Jake cleared his throat again.

'Of course, there's no point me making a rule for other people and not abiding by it myself. So tonight, I'm handing in my gun.'

He lifted out his pearl-handled Colt

.45 and laid it on the table in front of Jeremiah Isaacs.

'I reckon we can run this town without these. I guess that's all I have to say.'

Jake sat down again behind the table. The room was silent and then, someone clapped. A few more people joined in and one or two men rose to their feet. Soon the whole room was clapping and cheering. Neville and Jeremiah leaned over and patted Jake on his back and, before they knew what was happening, men were walking forward, removing their gunbelts and placing them on the table until it looked like an armory.

Elaine made her way through the milling crowd of townsfolk and stood beside Jake. He looked down at her and smiled. She reached up on her toes and kissed him on his cheek.

'I'm very proud of you, Jake Chalmers — and your folks would be very proud of you too.'

'Thanks, Elaine. It's getting a little

crowded here, though. Want to go home?'

She nodded. Jake bade his farewell to Neville and Jeremiah and with difficulty the young couple made their way to the door through the crowd of well-wishers.

Outside, the evening was cool and the last of the sun was just about to dip below the horizon as they made their way down the quiet and peaceful main street of Sweetwater, where gun law would never rule again.

THE END

We do hope that you have enjoyed reading this large print book.

Did you know that all of our titles are available for purchase?

We publish a wide range of high quality large print books including:
Romances, Mysteries, Classics
General Fiction
Non Fiction and Westerns

Special interest titles available in large print are:
The Little Oxford Dictionary
Music Book, Song Book
Hymn Book, Service Book

Also available from us courtesy of Oxford University Press:
Young Readers' Dictionary
(large print edition)
Young Readers' Thesaurus
(large print edition)

For further information or a free brochure, please contact us at:
Ulverscroft Large Print Books Ltd.,
The Green, Bradgate Road, Anstey,
Leicester, LE7 7FU, England.
Tel: (00 44) **0116 236 4325**
Fax: (00 44) **0116 234 0205**

Other titles in the
Linford Western Library:

GANNON'S LAW

Peter Wilson

Sheriff Jim Gannon's wife-to-be, Kate, is killed by a sniper, triggering a chain of events that brings the lawman into a conflict with bullying Jack Clayton and his sons. Gannon is drawn into a web of treachery, robbery and murder, involving stolen Union gold and a mysterious renegade Confederate soldier — Clay McIntire. Gannon tracks down the outlaws and learns of their secret past. Then realizes, perhaps too late, that his life is in danger from friend and foe alike . . .

SILVER EXPRESS

Gillian F. Taylor

Sheriff Alec Lawson is riding on the Northern Colorado Railroad train when silver bullion, worth thousands of dollars, is stolen. He and his deputies search the mountains and mining camps for the thieves. Lawson is convinced it's no simple theft. Greed lies at the root of it all: bribes, bounties, social status and death. The Sheriff and his men risk all for other people's money, and death seems close when you ride on the roof of a runaway train!

READY FOR TROUBLE

Corba Sunman

When Clay Overman is shot at he suspects the worst; he has no idea who wants him dead. Then the stream, supplying water for the Bar O ranch, runs dry. Scheming men are intent on robbing him and his father of their ranch and their lives. In this lawless world everyone must fight to retain their possessions and Clay is ready for trouble. But when the shooting begins his life will be on the line until the last shot . . .